"What will it take for you to leave?"

Marc's steely gray eyes bored into hers, the bitterness in his tone was ill concealed. "I'll make you an offer."

Daniella didn't reply. Let him say what he wants.

"One hundred thousand dollars and a plane ticket to wherever you want to go."

Daniella ran her fingers along the crease of her trousers. Be calm now, she admonished herself. She glanced up at him, smiling absently. "No, thank you."

Marc jammed his hands into his pockets. "One hundred and fifty thousand."

There was a heavy silence, loaded with tension. A thought occurred to her. How far would Marc be willing to go?

KAREN van der ZEE is an author on the move. Her husband's work as an agricultural adviser to developing countries has taken them to many exotic locations. The couple said their marriage vows in Kenya, celebrated the birth of their first daughter in Ghana and their second in the U.S., where they make their permanent home. The whole family spent two fascinating years in Indonesia. Karen has had several short stories published in her native Holland, and her modern romance novels with their strong characters and colorful backgrounds are enjoyed around the world.

Books by Karen van der Zee

HARLEQUIN PRESENTS

708—GOING UNDERGROUND
798—STAYING CLOSE
830—PELANGI HAVEN
982—FANCY FREE
1126—SHADOWS ON BALI
1158—HOT PURSUIT
1222—BRAZILIAN FIRE
1350—JAVA NIGHTS

HARLEQUIN ROMANCE

2334—SWEET NOT ALWAYS
2406—LOVE BEYOND REASON
2652—SOUL TIES

KAREN VAN DER ZEE

kept woman

Harlequin Books

TORONTO • NEW YORK • LONDON
AMSTERDAM • PARIS • SYDNEY • HAMBURG
STOCKHOLM • ATHENS • TOKYO • MILAN

Harlequin Presents first edition December 1991
ISBN 0-373-11422-2

Original hardcover edition published in 1991
by Mills & Boon Limited

KEPT WOMAN

CHAPTER ONE

SOMETHING was wrong.

Daniella stared down at her plate of food, seeing nothing. She speared a shrimp with her fork and brought it to her mouth. Her hand trembled. She heard the hubbub of voices around the large table, distinguishing nothing. Classical music hovered delicately in the background. Expensive perfumes mingled in the air.

He hadn't looked at her—not once.

She couldn't eat; her stomach was twisting itself into knots. She put the fork down, wiped her mouth with the white linen napkin and took a small sip of the wine. Marc was sitting at the other side of the long table, a few seats down. He had slipped in late, attempting to seat himself unobtrusively. His plane must have been delayed; he should have been home hours ago.

All day she'd been nervously waiting for him, looking in the mirror, wondering if he'd find her changed. She had changed, of course, in many ways. She looked more sophisticated now, her blonde hair framing her face in a curly halo, her make-up more professional, making her eyes look larger and a deeper blue. Every time she heard a car coming up the long drive, her heart would leap crazily in her chest.

She took another sip of her wine, glancing casually across the table over the rim of her glass. It had been three years since she'd last seen Marc and he still looked just as she remembered him—big and rugged and untamed, with thick black hair and magnetic grey eyes in a darkly tanned face.

5

He had tried to be unobtrusive, but of course it had been impossible. He stood out in this fashionable crowd of Washingtonians with their elegant clothes, their carefully trimmed and coiffed heads, their polished smiles. Not that there was anything wrong with his clothes—the dark suit, the white shirt and striped tie were impeccable and fitted his muscled body to perfection. But the unruly mop of dark hair, the roughly hewn features of the bronzed face and the slightly disdainful expression of the pale eyes as they swept around the room marked him as an outsider.

They'd all noticed him. Talking and asking questions, they were barely giving him a chance to eat his dinner. Was Africa really as dangerous a spot as the newspapers said? they asked. He said it depended where you were, given the fact that the continent had over fifty countries—some of them as peaceful as your own back yard.

For minutes after he'd arrived Daniella had sat motionless in her chair, watching him with her heart in her throat, waiting for him to notice her. But he hadn't looked at her—his grey eyes had moved over her as if she weren't there, as if she was invisible. Something was wrong. She didn't understand—why was he ignoring her? Had he forgotten? No, it wasn't possible. Three years was a long time, but not long enough to forget. Yet he had never written or called. Even at Christmas there'd been no word from him, not even for his father.

'I understand Marc has come home to join the company,' the man next to her commented. He was overweight and carefully groomed, his toupee a masterful arrangement of deception.

'I don't know,' she said, smiling with an effort. She doubted it very much. Hayden would have told her.

'Surely Hayden has told you,' Carl Burgess said, winking at her.

She felt herself grow rigid, ready to give the creep a swipe across the face to wipe out the leering expression. It was definitely something she'd have done in her earlier life—something in fact that she had done. But not now, at this elegant table, in this large, beautiful house owned by one of the richest men in the Washington D.C. area. She was a lady now, wearing an expensive silk dress, making charming conversation with Hayden's guests. This was an important dinner; she would have to behave herself. Poor orphan Annie she was no longer.

So she produced a gracious smile. 'Actually, we have not discussed it, Mr Burgess.' She pretended to concentrate on her food, not wanting to continue the conversation. She couldn't taste a thing, which was too bad because the food was beautiful and delicious, as it always was at Hayden's dinners. He preferred to entertain at home rather than in restaurants or hotels, which was more common among the well-to-do in Washington.

She glanced at Hayden, wondering what he felt about the return of his son. He had said little about it in the last few days and she wasn't sure what he was thinking. She knew not all was well with their relationship and it made her sad to think that perhaps something was seriously wrong.

Again her gaze settled on Marc. His hair was too long. For spring he seemed impossibly tanned. He looked restless—like a lion in a cage. He was listening to the woman on his right, a rather matronly type adorned with diamonds. Daniella could tell by the deadly polite expression on his face that his mind was not being greatly stimulated. After spending three years in West Africa working on a large engineering project, he no doubt had trouble finding great interest in the latest Washington gossip.

His gaze wandered, slipping right over her face on to the next person as if he didn't recognise her, didn't even see her. Her stomach tightened, a rush of heat pumped through her blood, and her hands went clammy. She could feel her body trembling.

Plates were removed quietly. Dessert was served: gold-edged plates with something creamy white floating in a red raspberry sauce. She managed to eat a few spoonfuls, wishing she could just leave and hide in her room, but of course that was not a possibility. Damn him, she thought suddenly, feeling anger displace the nervous tension. Damn him for doing this to me! Who does he think he is to ignore me like this?

He was Hayden Penbrooke's son, that was who he was. He could do whatever he pleased. He had always done whatever he pleased. That was why he'd become an engineer rather than a businessman. That was why he'd spent years in Africa rather than join his father's company.

Three years ago, after she'd first moved into Hayden Penbrooke's house, Marc had not ignored her. In those days he... Daniella stopped herself. She didn't want to think about that any more, about that one happy, delirious month. She'd made the mistake of thinking about it too much too often. It was nothing. It was history. A passing fancy.

Why then did she feel so miserable? Why then did she want to go up to Marc and shake him? It's me! she wanted to shout. Don't you recognise me?

She took a deep breath. This was ridiculous; she was making too much out of this. She was blowing this way out of proportion. After all, it was now three years later and life had moved on.

She struggled through the rest of the evening, pretending to listen, pretending to be charming and gracious and full of laughter and cheer. The party moved to the large sitting-room for coffee. A fire crackled cheerfully in the fireplace, the curtains had been drawn. It was a beautiful room, with large, deep sofas and comfortable chairs, and exquisite Persian carpets covering the gleaming oak floor. A small grouping of photographs in silver frames was displayed on the sideboard. They were pictures of the family in earlier years: Hayden with his beautiful wife, Marc as a boy hugging his dog, and blonde, blue-eyed Melissa—his younger sister who had died tragically at the age of fifteen. Six years ago Hayden had lost his wife and Marc his mother; wealth was no insurance against misfortune and grief. It was odd, how she had always assumed the rich could solve all their problems with money.

When finally the last guests had left, Daniella got to her feet—she could no longer bear to sit in front of the large fire with only Hayden, and Marc who'd been studiously avoiding speaking to her or looking at her.

Hayden stood up too, putting an arm around her shoulders. 'Are you all right?' His warm brown eyes looked concerned. 'You look pale.'

'I have a headache,' she said, which was the truth, if only a partial one.

He put a hand to her forehead. 'You feel warm.'

She was touched by his concern and she forced a smile. 'It's from the fire. I'll be all right, really. I'll take some aspirin.' She was self-consciously aware of Marc sitting in a chair nearby, observing them.

Hayden kissed her cheek. 'Go to bed. Sleep.'

She smiled. 'I will. Goodnight.'

Slowly she moved up the large, curving staircase, holding the skirt of her dress so as not to trip over it. On the landing she paused for a moment; she was tired, as if she'd spent the day digging ditches. On the floor below, the sitting-room door opened. She glanced down, seeing Marc coming up the stairs, taking the steps two at a time. Her heart jumped into her throat.

He stood in front of her, tall and overpowering. His clear grey eyes focused on her face, looking at her for the first time that evening. 'I want a word with you,' he said.

Her hands clenched into fists. She felt small and ridiculously vulnerable; five foot three wasn't much and next to Marc Penbrooke it was nothing. She straightened her back and looked at him coolly. 'So you *do* know who I am?'

'Oh, yes,' he said meaningfully, 'I do know who you are.' He looked her up and down, his eyes contemptuous. 'Very beautiful, very elegant.' It sounded like an insult.

She didn't know what was going on, why he acted the way he did. She stared at him, silent.

His hand reached out and one finger touched her necklace—the gold chain ending in a knot with a diamond in its centre.

'Diamonds,' he said. 'From my father, I presume?'

She swallowed. 'Yes, he gave it to me for my twenty-first birthday.' Hayden had given it to her along with the matching earrings: small knots with smaller diamonds. She'd been overwhelmed by the gift, had not felt right about accepting it, but he'd made it impossible not to.

'Today is special,' he'd said. 'You're twenty-one and every girl needs some jewellery.' He'd fastened the necklace around her neck and smiled.

'I've never had anything like it,' she'd whispered.

Hayden had lightly touched the sparking stone, as Marc was doing now. 'You're the diamond,' he'd said in an oddly quiet tone.

The image of herself as the diamond, encircled and held by the knot of gold—the symbol of Hayden's love and caring—had brought tears to her eyes. 'Oh, Hayden, it's beautiful,' she'd said, hugging him as she'd felt the tears spill over and run down her cheeks.

He'd held her tight. 'You don't know how much you mean to me,' he'd said, his voice full of emotion.

She'd smiled through her tears. 'You're the best thing that ever happened to me.'

Biting her lip, Daniella looked at Marc. She would never forget her twenty-first birthday.

Marc removed his finger from the diamond. 'A love-knot,' he said sarcastically, 'how touching.'

Anger washed over her. How dared he use that tone of voice? Who did he think he was? He knew nothing, *nothing*! She clenched her hands into fists. 'Will you please tell me what's going on here?'

His jaws tensed. 'You know exactly what's going on here.'

She glared at him. 'I'm not going to stand here and play guessing games! Either you come to the point or I'm going to bed. I'm tired and I have a headache. It's been a long night.'

He shoved his hands into his pockets, eyes cold. 'All right,' he said slowly and carefully. 'I'll come to the point: I want you to pack up your things. I want you out of this house.'

CHAPTER TWO

SHE stared at him, then gave a disbelieving laugh. 'You're out of your mind.'

'Oh, no,' he drawled. 'I'm quite sane. I want you out of my father's house.'

How dared he? How dared he tell her to leave this house, leave his father? What kind of son was *he*, always on the go? No phone calls, no letters, no visits in three years. He was an only son and he ignored his father. All her defences rallied in furious haste. Her spine went rigid and she looked at him coolly.

'This is not your house: I don't believe it's any of your business whether I live here or not.'

Steely grey eyes bored into hers. 'I'll make it my business. You may be taking advantage of my father, but you won't have that luck with me.'

Despair mingled with the anger, making her knees shake. Not him too. Not Marc, like all the others.

Maybe it was not meant to be—maybe she simply was not meant to be happy and live a decent life. Yet, so far, she had ignored the rumours and the gossip columns in the paper, as Hayden had told her to do. But with Marc it was different: he was not a stranger, not someone easily ignored. She felt rebellion stiffen her muscles. She had the right to her life, no matter what Marc thought. It was none of his business! She took a deep breath and anchored her feet to the floor to steady herself. Calm yourself now, she admonished herself. Don't let him see how you feel.

She looked right into the cold, grey eyes. 'May I ask you for a reason?' Her voice was beautifully controlled; she was proud of herself.

His mouth curved contemptuously. 'Don't ask for the obvious.'

His mind was already made up, his judgement obvious. It was in his eyes and in the tone of his voice. Nothing she said would make any difference—she was quite sure of that. He would not believe her. Inside her she could feel the old forces gathering: pride and self-respect and belief in herself. She was tough, she was strong—she'd learned to be early in life.

She was calm now, very calm; she would give Marcus Penbrooke his money's worth.

She smiled cheerily. 'Perhaps I'm dense—you may be overestimating my intelligence.' She flicked a curl away from her face. 'I'm just a dizzy blue-eyed blonde, you do realise that. Pray tell why you want me out of this house.'

His eyes narrowed dangerously. 'I want you away from my father.'

She gave him a wide-eyed look of surprise. 'Why?'

His eyes were like steel. 'Playing innocent, are we?'

'Innocent? I don't understand. What am I supposed to be guilty of? Surely I have the right to know what heinous crimes I'm charged with?'

'Do you really want this to be long and ugly? Why don't you get out while the going is good?'

She shook her head regretfully. 'I've no intentions whatsoever of leaving—I'm quite happy here, thank you.'

He didn't know how happy. For the first time in her life she felt she had a home, a place to belong. She wasn't leaving, no way, no how. Not until Hayden himself sent her away, and she knew he wouldn't.

'Oh, you'll leave,' he said, his voice ominously calm. 'I'll make sure of it.'

She shrugged casually. 'You still haven't told me why.'

He crossed his arms in front of his chest. 'You've insinuated yourself into this house. You're taking advantage of my father's generosity.'

'Oh, I see! Your father needs protection; people take advantage of him so easily.' The idea was laughable—nobody, but nobody took advantage of Hayden Penbrooke.

His mouth twisted. 'Not many, I'm sure. But you are young and very beautiful and you haven't got a cent to your name. Hayden is a lonely old man; he is also a very wealthy old man. Do I need to say more?'

'Oh, by all means, go on! It's getting very interesting.' It was getting easier already, playing the part.

His jaw went rigid. 'You're as hard as stone, aren't you?'

She nodded in agreement. 'You get that way when your own grandfather beats you up and you live with rats and cockroaches for a few years.'

'Spare me your sob stories.'

She shrugged. 'Sure, anything. Just tell me why you want me to leave and why it's so important to you. It's still not entirely clear to me. Can you explain it to me in twenty-five words or less? In plain English?'

His mouth tensed. 'You want plain English? I'll give you plain English. You are my father's mistress. If you can hold on long enough, maybe he'll marry you, maybe he'll put you in his will.'

'Money.' She let out a long-suffering sigh. 'So that's what this is all about. Why didn't you say so in the first place?' She saw the flames of anger leaping in his eyes, but he didn't frighten her. 'Your concern for your father is truly touching. It couldn't possibly be inspired by just a teensy weensy touch of self-interest? Your father's wealth, I imagine, is considerable.'

'I'm sure you know it to the last cent,' he bit out.

'As a matter of fact, I don't: I don't give a damn about his money.'

'Of course not,' he said sarcastically. He raked his hands through his hair. 'Do you really think he's going to marry you?'

He almost made her laugh. 'No.'

His eyes were chips of ice. 'So,' he said slowly, 'let me see if I have this straight—you're not interested in his money, or so you say, and you don't think he'll marry you. Then please tell me, why are you living with him?'

She looked straight into his eyes, pausing for effect. 'Because I love him,' she said.

And it was true—Hayden was the father she'd never had; the man who helped her with her career, encouraged her, applauded her. And she hadn't insinuated herself into his house—Hayden had taken her there himself and then asked her to stay. Please, he had said, this house needs some young blood. It's too big and too empty for an old man like me. There's plenty of room and you'd be doing me a favour.

Of course, he had known she was alone and had no money, that she had dreams and ambitions that would be easier realised if she had a place to live. It had not taken Daniella long to discover that Hayden was lonely, that he still grieved for his dead wife and that the pain of losing his daughter would always be with him. She hoped that in some small way she was alleviating his loneliness.

Marc's face was a mask of mockery. 'You love him,' he said sarcastically.

'Yes.' She straightened and turned away; she'd had enough of this conversation. She'd had enough of Marc Penbrooke and she was going to bed.

A wave of fatigue washed over her, mingled with a dull despair. This was not how she had expected this evening to be; she'd looked forward to Marc's return home, more than she would even admit to herself in rational moments. She'd dreamed about him, seeing again his bright, smiling eyes which lightened her heart, chasing away all the shadows which darkened her life. Thinking about him, she'd remembered all the good times they'd had and fantasised about what might happen when he returned from Africa. Juvenile dreams, naïve thoughts. She should have known better, should have been wiser. She swallowed hard.

An iron hand clamped around her wrist. 'Don't you leave.'

She stared at him hard. 'Take your hand off me. Now!'

He stared back into her eyes and suddenly the silence vibrated around them. She felt his grasp relax as something changed in his expression, subtly, and her heart contracted. Tears blurred her vision.

She felt his mouth on hers, his arms around her. A desperate, hungry kiss and for a wild, joyous moment the whole nightmarish evening fell away and three years were gone. She was in his arms again, strong arms that held her so easily, arms that made her feel so safe, so wanted. She felt transported on the wings of memory, back to that magical landscape of their first kiss—the virginal white world of the gardens after a surprise spring snowfall. So beautiful, so full of wonder and romance. His dark hair was flecked with white snowflakes; his eyes, shining with silvery lights, smiled at her and her heart leaped with delicious anticipation. Warmth rose to her cheeks and it was suddenly hard to breathe. He was so close, so close.

His warm mouth sent her blood surging hotly through her body. Her breasts pressed against his hard chest and long-buried need uncurled treacherously inside her. Her hand crept up, her fingers lacing themselves into the thick curly hair at the back of his head.

'Daniella?' It was nothing more than a whisper, yet the sound of his voice shattered the stillness of the dream.

Sanity returned. She tore herself away, appalled, furious.

'You bastard,' she whispered fiercely. 'You rotten bastard!' She whirled around and swung away down the hall to her room, pretending not to see the stunned expression in his grey eyes.

She sat on the edge of the big bed, trembling, taking in deep gulps of air. It was dark in the room, with only the pale grey light of a cold moon sneaking in through the window. She couldn't remember the last time she'd been so upset—such a painful mixture of anger and despair. But she had to keep herself under control. She was good at that—she'd learned a lot in her childhood, if not necessarily the normal sort of things.

Slowly she began to take control. She tried her legs; they felt steadier. She turned on the bedside lamp and a soft rosy glow filled the room. Her room, her sanctuary.

She kicked off her shoes, feeling the deep, luxurious pile of the cream carpet under her feet. It was a large, beautiful room, with a view of the gardens and the woods beyond. In the daytime, squirrels chased each other up and down the thick trunks of the old oak trees that shaded the house and lawn, and a multitude of birds which were fed from the feeder Daniella had installed outside her window. There was a big, comfortable bed, lovely furniture, green plants. The room was decorated in dusky rose and ivory and it was the most beautiful room she'd ever had. Not that it was so important to have a beautiful room—there were other things much more important—but it was nice and comforting just the same. She walked to the connecting door, opened it and turned on the light. This room was more important yet.

She surveyed the large, bright space, the huge windows and skylights, dark now against the night sky. An easel stood near the window with the acrylic painting she'd been working on for the last few days. She had a big work-table for doing her water-colours and there were shelves stocked with paints and other supplies. This was her most treasured possession: her very own painting studio so she could do what she wanted to do more than anything else in the world.

She'd fantasised, in these last few days, of bringing Marc here to show him her paintings. He would admire her work and see how much she had improved. When she'd first come to the house, three years ago, she'd had a few of her water-colours with her and she'd shown them to him, hesitant, fearful that she would see only politeness in his eyes as his mouth would say something nice. But it hadn't been the case—his admiration had been real. He'd especially liked one painting of a field of dandelions—sunny yellow spheres glowing bright in a green lawn. *Love*, she'd titled it.

'*Love?*' he'd asked softly, puzzled. 'When I think of love I think of....'

'Roses?' she finished for him.

He smiled. 'Yes. Dandelions are...weeds.' He sounded almost apologetic.

'And everyone is always out to destroy them.'

His eyes were thoughtful, then he smiled. 'And they always come back.'

'Yes.' Her face was warm, her heart beating erratically. 'You can't destroy true love, no matter what you do to it.'

'You're right,' he said quietly, looking intently at the picture. 'They're beautiful, actually, aren't they? I never really noticed.'

She was ridiculously pleased with his words. Dandelions were beautiful. Sometimes people had trouble seeing the beauty of the most ordinary things. Later, she had framed the painting, carefully wrapped it and given it to him as a present to take with him to Africa.

In the back of her mind she'd had fantasies of going with him and living a wildly exotic life in darkest Africa. She'd dreamed of being with him, of being inspired by love as well as exciting, alien sights and making wonderful paintings. But these were merely fantasies and she'd understood it well enough.

On the day of his departure he'd hugged her hard against his chest. 'I only wish I'd met you sooner,' he'd said huskily.

Daniella bit her lip, pushing back the feelings of sadness and loss. She wondered what had happened to the painting. She closed the studio door gently and moved over to the mirror. She looked at her reflection, at the exquisite silk dress, the beautiful Italian shoes. Even now, sometimes she couldn't believe it was really her—this elegant woman looking back at her from the mirror. A new life, a new incarnation of this scruffy blonde-haired little girl who grew up poor, in a dry, desolate town, with a mother who barely managed to scrape by on the meagre earnings of a waitress in a roadside café, and a grandfather—a bitter old man who drank too much.

Reaching behind her, she pulled down the long zip-fastener of her dress and let it slip to the floor with a soft whisper of silk. She bent down to retrieve it and hung it away in the large wardrobe.

'Beautiful', 'elegant'—Marc's words came back to her through the silence. It was, of course. It was dreadfully expensive as well, but paid for with her own money, not Hayden's. She'd bought it only a few days ago, wondering what Marc would think when he saw her, hoping he would still...

'Damn you, Marcus Penbrooke,' she muttered to herself, feeling tears burn behind her eyes. She forced them back—she didn't care what he said or what he did. She wasn't leaving; she was staying here, with Hayden.

She got ready for the night and lay in bed, thinking and remembering, wondering what or who had poisoned Marc's mind.

Only Hayden was at the breakfast-table when Daniella came down to the sun-lounge the next morning. She let out a slow sigh of relief; she wasn't ready to deal with Marc so early in the morning.

'How are you feeling?' Hayden asked, putting down the paper.

She smiled. 'I'm fine. The headache's all gone.' He looked fine himself, too. At sixty-nine he was amazingly fit and energetic. He was a big man—like Marc—still very straight, with an abundance of silver-grey hair. One day Marc would look like his father, but perhaps not quite so distinguished. Marc was a little too rugged for the polished gentleman look.

'Are you going in to work today?' Hayden asked.

She poured herself some coffee and nodded. 'We're hanging the Keiler show and I promised to be there today.' She buttered a piece of toast.

'Put some honey on it!' he ordered. 'You need the calories.'

She laughed. 'I like it this way, you know that.'

'You'll be skinny for the rest of your life.'

'I'm not skinny.'

He sighed. 'You need to eat a decent breakfast.'

'I'm not hungry in the mornings.'

It was the same conversation they had every now and then: he would say the same things and she would give him the same predictable answers. She smiled to herself— it must satisfy the latent parent in him. He wanted to take care of her, but she didn't resent it; even now, at twenty-three, it felt good to have someone care about her. Someone who was concerned when she had a headache, someone who cared what she ate. Small things, yet to her they were the touches of love.

'What about you?' she asked. 'What are you doing today?'

'Board meeting.' He frowned. 'I'll be late tonight. You and Marc can go ahead and eat—don't wait for me— I'll probably have dinner in town.'

She took a sip of coffee and tried to look casual. 'What are Marc's plans, do you know? Will he be home for a while or is he off to some other place again soon?'

The handsome face tightened. 'He has another offer he's looking into. Ghana again, he said.'

She wondered if Hayden had hoped Marc was home to stay, to help him run the company, to take over even- tually. She felt a tightening in her chest; something was not right between father and son, but she didn't know the details. Hayden seldom mentioned his son and he had never explained what exactly was wrong. Still, Marc was home now, staying in his father's house. There had to be hope, some chance of reconciliation. Surely Marc realised his father was getting older and that he needed his son?

She bit into her toast, chewing it slowly. What would happen if she told Hayden that Marc had told her to leave the house? It wasn't really a question—she knew very well what would happen: Hayden would not tolerate that kind of interference in his private life—not from anybody, not even his own son. He would blow up. There would be the confrontation of all confrontations and the rift between father and son would be complete. Marc would leave and never come back. She didn't want that on her conscience. If Marc wanted to ruin his relationship with his father, he'd have to do it on his own. She wanted no part of it.

She finished her coffee and pushed her chair back. 'I'd better be off.' She put a hand on his shoulder and kissed him on the cheek. 'Don't work too hard.'

He scowled at her and she laughed. 'OK, OK, do work hard. Have a ball.'

'I will.'

She wiggled her fingers at him and swung out of the room, smiling. He didn't like her telling him things like 'don't work too hard', 'take it easy', or 'be careful'. It was advice for fools, he said. Yet he'd turn around and say the same thing to her! When she pointed this out to him, he'd say it wasn't the same thing. It wasn't the same thing, of course, because she was a woman and he was a man. He was a male chauvinist—but she found it easy to forgive him.

She turned the corner and almost ran headlong into Marc's broad chest. She stepped aside hastily, feeling the smile fade from her face.

'Cheerful, aren't we?' he asked, obviously aware of her change of expression. 'Is my father in there?' He motioned towards the sun-lounge.

'Yes.'

Marc was dressed in a blue jogging suit and had apparently just come in from a run. He looked cold and dishevelled, his hair damp with sweat. After living in the tropics, the cool air of a spring morning must have chilled him to the bone. One part of her wanted to ask, the other part wanted to just get away. Marc wasn't Marc; he wasn't the same man she'd known three years ago.

'You're up early,' he said, as if it surprised him.

'So are you,' she shot back.

'There's something we need to discuss,' he stated, giving her an appraising look.

'I don't think we have anything to discuss at all.' She tried to move past him, but he blocked her way.

'Oh, yes, we do.'

She shrugged. 'All right, but it will have to wait. I'm on my way out.' He looked alarmingly fit and masculine and she wished she wasn't so acutely aware of his male appeal.

He lifted a mocking eyebrow. 'Shopping?'

'At seven in the morning? The stores don't open until ten.'

'True. I forgot.' He leaned lazily against the wall. 'So, where are you off to?'

'Work.'

Dark eyebrows rose. 'Work? How very virtuous.'

She stared at him. 'What is the matter with you?' she asked, sorry as soon as she uttered the words; she could hear the genuine concern in her own voice, the regret. She didn't recognise this man, she didn't understand his behaviour.

He laughed, a sound devoid of amusement. 'Nothing is the matter with me, thank you, but there is something the matter with my father, obviously.' He moved away from the wall. 'We'll discuss it later.'

She didn't answer, just moved past him down the hall and up the curved staircase to get her coat and bag. Five minutes later she drove her little white Mazda down the drive, catching sight of Marc standing in the sun-lounge window, watching her leave. She began to laugh suddenly, out loud, in the car. She was such a fool! How could she have attached so much importance to something that had happened so long ago? Well, she hadn't, not really. Knowing Marc was coming home had just stirred up the memories, but actually she'd quite forgotten him. So much had happened in the last few years and Marc was of no importance whatsoever. It was just one more illusion down the drain. She was used to that too. She'd had lots of dreams and illusions in her life and she'd had to give up most of them. But there were always other ones to take their place and, now and then, they even became reality. Like her life now with Hayden, her home, her painting. Hayden was the best thing that had ever happened to her.

And now Marc wanted her to leave; he wanted her to release his father from her *femme fatale* clutches. She laughed again—it was too funny for words. Just let him try! She was used to fighting—it might even be fun. She turned on the radio. A cheerful reggae tune danced into the air, filling the car with its rhythmic sounds. She sang along, loud and happily, as she drove down the George Washington Parkway, seeing the new leaves sprouting in glorious celebration of spring. Dogwoods bloomed white and pink and the grass was so green it hurt her eyes. For a moment all the colours blurred; she blinked hard. Spring was so beautiful.

* * *

'So tell me all about it,' Anne said, trying not to sound too eager. She was taking the Keiler paintings out of their wooden crate, throwing around foam and cardboard with happy abandon, like a child destroying a room. She had a mass of curly auburn hair and big brown eyes. Anne always wore black. Black was supposed to be artistic, especially combined with exotic scarves and 'ethnic' jewellery. Anne ran the Benedict Gallery, taking her orders from Andrew Benedict—the owner. Daniella worked two days a week and had done so for three years. The rest of the time was hers to paint and to take classes at the Corcoran School of Art. She liked working at the Benedict, meeting the artists and seeing their work.

Her own paintings were on display in various places: a few art shops and—thanks to Hayden—in a couple of banks, a lawyer's office, and the showroom of a prestigious interior design company. Especially in the last year, she had been selling better than she'd dared hope.

Daniella looked at Anne. 'The dinner-party was a big success. I'm sure Hayden will get what he wants—he always does.'

Anne glowered. 'To hell with the party! I want to know about The Man.'

'Oh, him.'

'How was he?'

'Very tanned.'

Anne threw a piece of packing foam at her. 'Did you have a night full of wild, passionate love?'

Daniella grimaced. 'It was wild and passionate all right, sort of.'

'What do you mean, sort of?'

'He told me, in quite passionate terms, to get the hell out of his father's house. He thinks I'm having an affair with his poor demented father and I'm going to worm my way into his will and take all the loot!'

Anne almost choked. 'Oh, lord, where did he get that idea?'

Daniella gave her a disparaging look. 'Come on, Anne. Same place everybody else gets that idea.'

'But he was in Africa, for God's sake!'

'It's a small world.'

Anne lifted out one of the paintings. 'So what are you going to do?'

'Stay put.' Daniella took the painting and carefully leaned it against the wall. She stepped back and examined it. 'This is truly ugly.'

'Keiler's soul is truly ugly, so what do you expect?' Anne had had a short and disastrous affair with the artist the previous summer. It rather coloured her perceptions. Viciously she ripped out another piece of cardboard, then, more gently, lifted out another frame. 'Now look at this one. The devil made him do it.'

'I hope he doesn't sell a single painting,' Daniella said generously, in full support of her friend.

Anne grinned. 'And I hope you sell all yours.'

Daniella grimaced. 'I wish, I wish.'

'You're not nervous, are you?'

'Me? Hell, no. It's my first show, in the Nation's Capital, no less—why should I be nervous?'

Anne shook her head. 'Can't imagine.'

Daniella couldn't believe her good fortune; being part of a group show at the Benedict was a dream come true, a stroke of good luck that had come out of the blue. She wasn't nervous—she was terrified!

'What are you going to do?' Anne asked.

'About what?'

Anne sighed. 'About Marc.'

Daniella bit her lip and stared unseeingly at the painting in her hand. 'Nothing,' she said flatly, feeling a dull ache somewhere in the region of her heart.

It was dark when she arrived home and it had rained all the way—a stark contrast to the sunny weather of that morning. She was exhausted and all she wanted was to relax, go to bed early and watch something fluffy on TV. She was tempted to eat in the kitchen with Mrs Bell and Cora Lee, but she didn't want to give Marc the idea that she was avoiding him.

She showered quickly and changed into comfortable slacks and a periwinkle-blue sweater of soft angora wool. She brushed out her hair, then shook her head gently to let the curls fall more naturally. She examined herself in the mirror, looking back into large blue eyes accentuated by the colour of the sweater. It always amazed her to see herself looking so young and innocent—she didn't feel young and innocent. There had been times when she'd felt quite ancient, but never quite ancient enough to give up. She grimaced at herself in the mirror—no matter what her appearance might suggest, she was tough and stubborn and she didn't give up. Daniella Michaels never gave up.

She turned away from the mirror and determinedly moved to the door. She was going downstairs, into the dining-room, and she was going to have dinner with Marc.

He was already there, standing near the window, with a glass in his hand. He wore close-fitting jeans and a green and blue flannel shirt with the sleeves rolled up; wearing formal clothes had never been one of his priorities. He looked at ease with himself and disturbingly virile, even from the back. He turned when he heard her enter. His eyes narrowed as his gaze flickered over her.

She tried not to be intimidated by his scrutiny, tried not to let herself react to the masculine appeal of his big, muscular torso and strong brown hands. 'Hello,' she said cheerfully. 'It's bad out there.' Rain splattered against the panes and the wind howled around the corners of the house. It had been a night like this when Hayden had taken her home with him—the night she'd first met Marc. She wondered if he still remembered. If he still remembered her sitting at the kitchen table, wet and bedraggled, eating a roast beef sandwich Mrs Bell had made for her.

'I'll close the curtains,' he said, and proceeded to do so before moving to the bar. 'Would you like a drink?'

'A glass of white wine, please.'

He poured it for her and she took the glass, careful not to touch his fingers.

She smiled. 'Thank you.'

He did not smile back. He was going to be painfully polite, painfully civilised. She hoped she'd make it through the meal.

The door opened and Cora Lee entered with a tray. Cora Lee was nineteen and had recently been hired to help Mrs Bell, the cook, in the kitchen. She had a shiny cap of very short black hair, enormous dark eyes and favoured large, dangling earrings.

'Shark fin soup,' she announced. 'Mrs Bell says it's delicious, but it smells disgusting, if you ask me.' They sat down at the table and Cora Lee placed the soup plates in front of them, giving Marc a coquettish smile. 'You don't have to eat it if you don't want it.'

'I'll eat it.'

She put a hand on her hip. 'Maybe you're used to this stuff, living in Africa and all. What do they eat over there?'

His mouth crinkled up. 'You don't want to know.'

'Sure I do. They eat this stuff?'

'No.' Amusement glinted in his eyes. 'They eat yam and plantain and cassava with a little soup or stew poured over it. If they're lucky they'll have a little meat or a fish head floating in it, eyeballs and all.'

'That's revolting!'

'It's food.'

Cora Lee shrugged philosophically. 'Well, rather you than me.' She turned and left the room with a seductive swing of her hips. Daniella watched her, biting her lip, and trying to suppress a smile. Had Hayden been in the room she wouldn't have dared do that.

She picked up her spoon and her eyes met Marc's.

'What's so funny?' he asked.

'Cora Lee. She's usually a bit more demure, or tries to be, at least.' She spooned soup into her mouth. Living in Hayden's house she'd learned to eat a lot of unfamiliar foods—foods she would once have classified as disgusting along with Cora Lee. She'd grown up on hot dogs and peanut butter sandwiches, branching out to hamburgers and the occasional piece of fried chicken if she got lucky.

'How's Mrs Bell?' he asked. 'I went to see her this morning, but she seemed a little cool.'

'She's fine.'

Mrs Bell had been the cook for the past eighteen years. She was in her sixties now and had no intention of quitting despite her arthritis. Hayden, not wanting to retire her against her will, had added Cora Lee to the staff which included a housekeeper and a cleaning girl. The housekeeper was a sour woman in her forties who moved through the house like a grey shadow. Daniella tried to avoid her, finding more agreeable company in the large, comfortable kitchen. At times, Daniella was still amazed to see all these people busy catering to two people living in the house. When she was only a little girl she'd done everything: cooking, cleaning, shopping, washing. Now she didn't do any of these things.

It wasn't a surprise to hear that Mrs Bell was a little 'cool' towards Marc. Although she'd never actually said it out loud, Daniella was well aware that Mrs Bell was of the opinion that Marc's place was with his father, that he shouldn't be tramping around the world when his father needed him. Mrs Bell thought the world of Hayden. He had adored his wife, who had died six years earlier. He was a warm, compassionate man, no matter what the newspapers said.

The soup was delicious and they ate it in silence. The main course was served: herbed rice and chicken in a mushroom and wine sauce. Daniella was grateful Marc didn't talk—it gave her an opportunity to gear herself up for the inevitable attack.

It came after the coffee had been brought in. He dropped a large envelope on to the table.

'Have a look at these.'

She took the envelope and opened it. There were news clippings in it, and photographs. She made a show of studying them, composing herself, pretending to be cool and detached. There was a photograph of Hayden and her at a charity ball. She was leaning towards him, whispering into his ear, and he was laughing. 'After years of loneliness, new love for Hayden Penbrooke,' the caption read. Another picture showed the two of them on the beach in St Barlow where Hayden owned a villa. Dressed in a blue swimsuit, Daniella was rubbing tanning oil into his back. 'Bliss in St Barlow Love Nest,' it said below. There were several articles giving juicy details of the love-life of the sixty-seven-year-old multi-millionaire property magnate and the penniless blonde beauty he had rescued from a life of privation. The implications were clear. She'd seen these articles, or similar ones. In the beginning

she'd been upset and angry, but later she'd simply ignored them.

She examined the envelope and met Marc's eyes.
'Somebody actually went through the trouble of sending
you these?'

'Yes.'

'Good heavens, you must have been hard up for
reading material if you read this smut!'

'I want you out of my father's house.'

She nodded. 'You mentioned that, yes. What is so
terrible about me living in this house? Why can't we have
dinner together? Keep each other company? Go out
together?'

'Sleep together?'

'Oh, is that what's bothering you? Yesterday it was
money, now it's sex. Such a potent mixture, isn't it?'

His face was as hard as stone. 'What's bothering me
is this entire set-up.'

She rested her arms on the table and leaned forward.
'Maybe it's none of your business. Has that possibility
occurred to you? Your father does not need your
protection; he is not a senile old man. If you'd stay
around more and work a little harder at being a real son
you would know that!'

The moment she uttered the words she knew she'd hit
a raw nerve. His stony expression crumbled. For a
moment a mixture of emotions fought for dominance—
anger, pain, and contempt.

' A "real son?"' The bitterness in his tone was ill-
concealed. 'What about him being a real father?' Marc
got to his feet, towering over her. 'But my relationship
with my father is not the issue here.'

'However, it's a very interesting one,' she said coolly.
'It might be worthwhile pursuing.' She was uncomfortably aware of the close proximity of his body, yet
determined not to show her unease.

Steely grey eyes bored into hers. 'What will it take for you to leave?'

'I'm not leaving.'

'Oh, yes you are.'

She sighed and leaned back in her chair, silent, waiting.

'You say you love my father.'

'Yes.'

'You must admit that's a little hard to swallow.'

She raised her eyebrows. 'Is it?'

'Yes. You are twenty-three years old and he is sixty-nine.'

'What does age have to do with love? He is a warm, loving man. He's considerate, charming and I enjoy his company.'

'You enjoy his money.' The words came swift and cold. 'Is that what you call love?'

She put her napkin down and moved her chair back, getting slowly to her feet. She held his eyes for a long, silent moment, trying hard not to feel the pain. 'Marcus Penbrooke,' she said slowly, softly, 'what do you know about love?'

Again, a raw nerve. A muscle jerked at his temple. She turned around, crossed to the door and left the room. She almost ran up the stairs, hearing the door below open and close. She went into her room, her heart pounding, but he was right behind her, striding straight into her room.

'Don't you walk out on me,' he said softly, dangerously.

'Get out of my room,' she said. 'You have no right.'

He laughed harshly. 'Let's not talk about rights, sweetheart.'

She bit her lip. It was stupid to have said that—no way could she make him leave and he knew it. It was even more stupid to have come up here in the first place; she should have stayed downstairs. But it was too late now—she'd just have to play it cool.

She shrugged carelessly. 'I thought we were finished.'

'We're not finished until you're out of here.'

She said nothing, looking at him with cool indifference.

He leaned against the door, hands in his jeans pockets, gazing around lazily. 'You've done well for yourself, haven't you? Nice place, nice clothes, nice car—not bad. Not bad at all.'

She did not reply. Let him say what he wanted; let him think what he wanted.

He moved over to the connecting door and opened it, switching on the light. 'Well, well, a studio. I remember reading about it. "The Millionaire and the Painting Beauty," or something like that.'

Daniella held her breath. She didn't want him to go in and look at her work. She would not be able to bear it if he looked at her paintings, mocking them perhaps and belittling them.

He stood in the doorway a moment longer, surveying the studio, then closed the door. Slowly she let out her breath. She sat down in a chair and curled her feet under her. She didn't know what was coming next, but she might as well be comfortable.

'I'll make you an offer,' he said.

She took an imaginary piece of fluff from her sweater, saying nothing.

'Are you interested?'

She shrugged. 'Sure.' She might as well play along with him, see what he had in mind.

'One hundred thousand dollars and a plane ticket to wherever you want to go.'

CHAPTER THREE

DANIELLA ran her finger along the crease of her trousers. Be calm now, she admonished herself. Don't let him get to you. She glanced up at him, smiling absently. 'No, thank you.'

His eyes narrowed. 'You bitch,' he said tightly.

She'd been called worse, but coming from him it hurt. She swallowed the pain and regained her composure. She raised her eyebrows in cool disdain. 'Why? Because I don't like your despicable offer?'

Marc jammed his hands into his pockets. 'One hundred and fifty thousand.'

'No,' she said stonily.

There was a heavy silence, loaded with quivering tension. A thought occurred to her. How far would Marc be willing to go? Why not play along with him? She examined her nails, feigning boredom. She was aware of his anger—it practically radiated from him in waves!

'I'll give you two hundred and fifty,' he said at last. 'My final offer—take it or leave it.'

A quarter of a million dollars. A tidy little sum, for sure. She glanced up. 'I know your father has that kind of money, but do you?'

'I'll get it. How about it, yes or no?'

She frowned, as if considering this. 'I'll need time to think about it.'

Triumph glittered in his eyes. 'I'll give you two days.'

She stared at him in challenge. 'Three days.' She'd stretch it as far as she could.

His eyes were grey ice, his face tightly controlled as if it took all his strength not to lose his temper. 'All right, three days.' He moved over to the door, his frigid gaze meeting hers. 'I suggest you accept the offer. The alternative may not be as profitable.'

The last thing she wanted was to dream of Marc, but she did—just as she had dreamed of him for months after he had left to go to Africa three years ago. In her dream he was familiar—the old Marc who had taken her to art galleries and museums, for drives in the Virginia countryside, to cosy little restaurants where her clothes didn't matter. She dreamed of the Marc who had held her and kissed her and made love to her.

'I love you,' he said in the dream. Strong arms around her. Loving arms, loving hands. Hands that caressed her. She couldn't remember ever being caressed. Her mother had been too tired, too sick. After she died, her grandfather had beaten her regularly for no reason that she'd ever understood. Until she'd decided that enough was enough and she'd walked out—taking his pay cheque, his antique gold watch, and two peanut butter sandwiches.

She'd been eighteen years old and for the next two years she'd lived in Richmond, working as a cocktail waitress at night and as a part-time model at a small art college in the daytime, soaking up whatever she could in terms of knowledge and technique. She'd lived in a drab little room with a tiny window, that overlooked a small courtyard crowded with overflowing garbage cans and empty boxes and crates. Dogs and cats would come to scavenge for food, and the ugly sounds of the animals fighting would often wake her at night. In the winter her room was cold, in the summer it was hot. She could have afforded a better place if she hadn't been determined to save every possible penny. She wanted to have enough money to go to Washington, go to art school and survive the first year. So she had scrimped and saved and finally boarded a Greyhound bus bound for Washington—a paradise of museums and art galleries she couldn't wait to visit.

In her dream it was all mixed up: images of her grandfather's drunken grin, the horrible little apartment, Marc kissing her, saying he loved her.

'I love you'. The words were still there when she awoke. It had only been a dream, she knew that—Marc had never said it, although she believed she'd seen love in his eyes. Maybe because she'd wanted it so badly. It might never really have been there at all. Maybe all she'd been then, three years ago, was an amusing diversion.

No, not even now could she believe that.

She spent the next day in her studio, painting, with the french doors open. The large house was built against a slope, giving the back of the second floor its own outside terraces. it was a balmy April day, the air clear and bubbly like effervescent spring water. She loved the sounds and smells of spring: the cheerful chorus of birds in the trees, the spicy scent of pines and green, growing things.

While she painted, she forgot everything, as if she had retreated into another world—a world of her own making. She was barely aware of the coming and going of Mrs Bell bringing her coffee, lunch, juice, some fruit. Sometimes painting was a welcome escape; she could withdraw from reality as she so often had done as a child. She had painted then to get away from the reality of an overworked mother and an abusive grandfather. On paper she would make up her own world with paint or crayons and pencils—a happy world of a child's imagination. Now, in the bright studio with the sounds of spring wafting in on the pine-scented breeze, she painted and forgot about Marc and the things he had said to her, forgot the pain and anger and indignation.

The daylight was beginning to fade when Hayden strolled by outside, puffing on his pipe. He stood in the doorway and smiled. 'I thought I might find you here. Mrs Bell says you haven't shown your face all day.'

Daniella put her brush down and sighed. 'I haven't any idea what happened to the time.' She raked a hand through her hair and stepped back to look critically at her work.

Hayden advanced into the room. 'May I see?'

She shook her head. 'Not yet—when it's finished.'

He laughed. 'How about some dinner first?'

'Oh, I won't finish it now—the light's going.' She didn't like painting by artificial light, although she did it sometimes. 'I'll change and I'll be down in ten minutes.'

'I'll pour you a drink.'

She smiled. 'Thanks. Could I have a sherry, please?'

'Anything your little heart desires.'

No, she thought with sudden sadness, not anything.

Marc and Hayden were standing by the bar, drinks in their hands, when she came down to the dining-room a little while later. Marc's eyes met hers briefly, impersonally, acknowledging her presence, which was something. He wore dark trousers and a blue sweater that made his tan look darker and his eyes even lighter. Her pulse quickened, which annoyed her no end. She did not want to feel this physical pull when her emotions were at war with him. Yet the conflict was there between the memories of the past and the realities of the present. Once this man had made love to her. Once she had seen him without the covering of clothes, seen the strong muscled legs, the flat stomach, the broad chest with the dark curly hair. Once he had seen her too, without clothes and kissed her breasts, making her body sing with his touch.

Warmth flooded her. Oh, God, she thought, what am I thinking? She bit her lip, hard. Hayden handed her a glass of sherry and she took it eagerly.

'We were talking about buying property in South Carolina,' he said.

'Commercial?' she asked, grateful for the distraction. Most of Hayden's properties were office complexes, hotels and shopping malls.

'Land allotted for luxury blocks of flats. Florida is overflowing with retired people and they're moving to South Carolina now.'

She sipped her sherry, feeling calmness returning. 'What do you think, Marc?' she asked, forcing him to look at her. Somehow, in the company of Hayden, they'd have to keep up a semblance of normality.

'I don't believe my views are relevant to my father's business goals.' His voice was coolly polite, but she sensed the tension underlying the statement.

'What are your views?'

His mouth twisted. 'I think he should go into low-income housing—there's a criminal shortage of it.'

Hayden stroked his chin. 'There's a reason for that, son.'

'I know. There's no money in low-income housing.'

'Exactly.'

Marc looked at his father, hard. 'You're almost seventy years old. How much more money do you want?'

Daniella held her breath. There was a loaded silence. She glanced at Hayden, afraid of what he might say. He puffed on his pipe, apparently unperturbed. 'It's not the money as much as it is the challenge of the game,' he said calmly.

Marc tossed back the last of his drink. 'Change the game, change the challenge.'

Hayden frowned, face pensive. 'Interesting thought,' he said.

Cora Lee came in with the first course, dark eyes lighting up when she noticed Marc. She smiled prettily as she set the plates of seviche on the table.

'Enjoy your meal,' she said demurely and made for the door. Passing Daniella, she leaned towards her. 'It's raw fish!' she whispered. 'It's disgusting!'

Daniella grinned. 'It's not raw,' she whispered back. 'It's been sitting in lime juice all day—it's pickled.'

They seated themselves at the table.

'What's so funny?' Hayden asked, looking at Daniella.

She laughed. Marc had asked the same thing the day before. 'Cora Lee is having a hard time with the disgusting food being served up in your house.'

Bushy eyebrows rose. 'Disgusting?'

'OK, exotic. Shark fin soup, seviche....'

'Well, we'll need to educate her. Have her try some.'

'Over her dead body.'

'You tried it?'

She grinned. 'Well, yes, I'm an adventurous person.' The truth was she would have eaten raw worms just to stay with Hayden. Fortunately, however, his culinary eccentricities had not yet reached that extreme.

Over the years Hayden's business activities had taken him to many places—familiar and foreign—and his love for eating, coupled with his natural curiosity, had added up to a diet of odd and sometimes bizarre foods.

Daniella examined the food on her plate. Pieces of white fish and shrimp, soaked in lime juice, lay nestled on a bed of lettuce surrounded by sliced avocado. She'd eaten seviche often, especially in the Caribbean where she and Hayden would go to stay in his villa on St Barlow a couple of times a year.

'Tell me about your show,' Hayden said. 'Have the invitations been sent out yet? And what about the advertising? Is Andrew taking care of that?'

Daniella grimaced. 'The ads are in, but the invitations will go out next week. It's a terrible rush job with everything having to be done at the last minute. Andrew is tearing his hair out. He's coming tomorrow to make the final selection.'

It was a chance of a lifetime to be able to show her work at the Benedict. The exhibit that had originally been scheduled had suddenly been cancelled. The artist— a fairly well-known painter from Arizona—was in hospital for major surgery and wasn't expected to recover in time for his show. To fill the time, Andrew had organised a group show of three promising young artists— a sculptor and two painters—and she, Daniella, was one of them.

It was too good to be true, wasn't it?

'I've watched you these last three years,' Andrew had said with a crooked grin. 'You're doing some very interesting and innovative work; you deserve a break.'

And a break it was. She'd walked on clouds for days until reality had hit her and panic had nearly claimed her. She needed paintings for the show, new paintings that had not been on display anywhere else. She had to get to work.

'You're not choosing your own paintings?' Hayden asked.

She grinned. 'One of Andrew's conditions was that he had a say in the selection. I don't think I'm in a position to be too arrogant at this point. I'm not going to push too hard, but I'll try to get him to pick what I want.'

'Try a little manipulation.'

She laughed. 'Shame on you!'

He patted her hand. 'Just make sure he takes the one of the little girl sitting at Jefferson's feet at the Memorial.'

They finished the seviche and Cora Lee brought in the main course. Marc hadn't as yet said a word. Well, Daniella thought, we must not make him feel like a stranger. She smiled at him.

'I've heard you might be coming home for good.'

He cocked one eyebrow. 'I don't know where you got that idea,' he said mildly.

She shrugged. 'Gossip. This town thrives on gossip.'

He ignored that and proceeded to eat.

'I also heard you're negotiating a new contract to go back to Africa. Is that true, then?'

'Yes.' He was not exactly a fountain of information!

'Is this for the same project, or are you starting something new somewhere else?'

He looked at her, face bland. 'It's for the second phase of the same project.'

'Water systems for small villages, isn't that it?'

'Right.' He cut a piece of his veal and brought it to his mouth, avoiding further talk.

Daniella was not ready to give up yet. 'I remember you telling me about it,' she went on. 'Clean water cuts down on water-borne disease, childhood dehydration, infant deaths. You said clean water is as important as food.'

He looked up, surprise flaring in his eyes. 'Yes.' For a moment his eyes held hers and the silence shivered with memories. Memories of long evenings in front of the fire, of walking hand in hand through an early spring snowfall. His eyes clouded and he looked down again at his plate and resumed eating.

She stared at his dark head, feeling a sudden painful regret. He had told her about the project three years ago and she'd been fascinated. Growing up in a rural town in the south of Virginia, she hadn't come across anyone who'd lived in Africa, anyone with such noble ambitions as bringing clean drinking-water to poverty-stricken African villages. He'd been so enthusiastic, so full of excitement, and she'd loved listening to him. He'd been the most intriguing man she'd ever met. They'd spent entire days together, laughing, talking. Now he didn't even want to see her. He didn't want to talk to her; he avoided her whenever possible. She didn't want it to hurt, yet it did.

No it doesn't, she told herself. Don't be a fool.

After dinner she escaped to her studio to tidy up. She'd had a good day and she was happy with her progress. She examined the painting more closely. It was good enough for her show.

A show at the Benedict. She closed her eyes and held her breath for a moment. It would give her wonderful exposure. It was exciting. It was terrifying.

After she'd cleaned up she examined her selection of paintings one more time, hoping Andrew would agree with her on the ones to use for the show. She felt exhilarated and nervous. Maybe a walk through the garden would take care of her excess of energy and calm her down. She stepped through the french windows on to the flagstone terrace.

The air was balmy and fragrant with the sweet perfume of lilac blossoms. She sniffed it appreciatively as she followed the flagstone path to the small pond in the back of the garden. Insects chirped in the grass. The blossoms of the dogwood shone white in the darkness. It was like a fairy-tale setting with the full moon gleaming silver in the dark sky. She would never get enough of spring.

She sat for a while on the wooden bench near the pond, feeling calmness returning, then slowly made her way back to the house, stopping near the lilac bushes for a moment, gently touching one of the blooms from a drooping branch.

There were footsteps on the path. Then a dark shape emerged, stood still. Even in the dark she knew who it was. Even now she felt her pulse leap—some primeval, instinctive reaction to the presence of a man—no, not any man, but a man who had once stirred her deeply. Somewhere deep inside her something still reacted to him, to a special part of him that might be lost forever. In the moonlight everything seemed different, as if the night had erased the sharp edges of shapes and feelings and words.

'Daniella?' The voice was soft. 'What are you doing out here in the dark?' His tone held no challenge.

'I like being out at night. It's so beautiful here. Do you smell the lilacs?'

'Yes.'

'Spring is magic.'

He moved closer. 'And so are you, aren't you?' he said quietly. 'In your white dress in the moonlight, your nose in the lilacs.' There was an odd tone to his voice—longing, regret. Or was she only imagining it? Yet she had not imagined the expression on his face at dinner, when she had surprised him by remembering the things he had told her about his work three years ago. For a moment, he too had been in the grip of the memories of those days.

She didn't know what to say. She let go of the bloom in her hand. Was it possible that the poison of gossip and prejudice had not reached all the hidden corners of his heart? Was there still some hope?

'I was watching you.' There was unmistakable hunger in his voice now. 'I was in my room and I saw you walk across the lawn.'

She tried to visualise what he had seen—a figure in white in the dark garden. Moonlight silvering the white dogwood blossoms. She could see it as a painting—mysterious, romantic. She closed her eyes, feeling a sense of unreality take over. They'd been together in this garden before, long ago, yet now as they were standing so close together it seemed only yesterday. She longed to reach out, touch him, feel his warm mouth on hers, his arms securely around her. This garden was a dreamland where wishes would come true because the moon was full and the lilacs were in bloom. Surely fairies were hiding in the shadows, watching the two of them and weaving around them a web of magic? His hand reached out and touched her hair, stroking it softly, then lacing his fingers through the curls, while his eyes, silver in the dark, locked with hers. She stood very still, forgetting to breathe. In the woods beyond the gardens, an owl hooted and suddenly the spell was broken, the magic gone. Marc's hand dropped away and his eyes clouded over.

He turned abruptly and strode away into the shadows of the night.

She felt oddly melancholy the next day and couldn't shake herself out of it. When Andrew called to say he was detained and wouldn't be able to come over to select the paintings, she didn't even mind.

Marc seemed to have disappeared. She saw nothing of him for the next couple of days and she felt a sinking feeling of regret. He was sorry about his weakness that night in the garden—a moment out of time when for an instant they had met in some other dimension. It hadn't changed his mind about her; he couldn't stand looking at her, so he made sure he didn't have to.

Damn him and his stupid assumptions! Damn her for caring!

'He's a bastard,' she said to Anne as they finished hanging the Keiler paintings. She had to talk to somebody; it was difficult to keep it all inside.

Anne frowned. 'He's still at it?'

'I don't know what he's up to. I don't understand what's the matter with him, why he can let himself be so taken in by those stories.' Daniella ran a hand wearily across her forehead. 'He never even asked me if any of it was true.'

The door to the gallery opened and in breezed Jade Devereaux, all smiling elegance. Dark, slanting eyes, sleek black hair. She greeted the two of them cheerfully, then frowned as she caught sight of the paintings on the wall. She moved a little closer, examining the works. 'Good God,' she said in a low voice. 'Where has he been?'

'To hell and back,' said Anne promptly, and Daniella laughed.

'At least,' Jade muttered.

'There are more in the other room,' Daniella said.

'No, thanks, I've seen enough.' Jade moved back to the counter. With a little leap she seated herself, swinging long, elegant legs. She wore a very short black skirt and a red silk blouse. 'Girls, how about a party?'

Anne's face lit up. 'Yeah,' she said, eagerly. 'Just what we need—a party. The gods are with us.'

Jade's parties were famous for being fun, and fun parties were a rarity in Washington. In the Nation's Capital, parties always had a purpose; they were the places where people congregated to do business or stir up trouble for the world—the hunting grounds of the movers, the manipulators, the opportunists and the power-brokers.

'We're going to have a psychic there,' Jade said.

'A *what*?' Daniella asked.

Jade eyes sparkled with humour. 'A psychic—she's famous in California and I ran into her last year. She can look right into the darkest corners of your soul.'

'Just what we need,' said Anne, grinning, 'somebody with spooky powers! Does she do spells? We badly need a spell!'

Jade gave her a disapproving look. '*Psychic* powers, not spooky—be careful now! And *no*, she does not do spells. She's not a common witch, for heaven's sake!'

Daniella laughed and Anne looked repentant. 'Sorry. I promise I won't ask for a spell. When's the party, anyway?'

Jade slipped off the counter and moved to the door. 'Next Saturday, eightish. I'm not sending invitations— they're such a waste of time.'

'We'll be there,' Daniella said. 'Thanks.'

Jade opened the door. 'I must be off. See you then!'

Anne sighed as she stared at the closed door. 'Boy, she leads a charmed life. She's got it all: money, beauty and a great husband.'

'In that order?'

Anne sighed again. 'I guess the great husband comes first. If I'd find a good one I wouldn't care about the rest.' She looked at Daniella. 'Would you?'

Daniella bit her lip, feeling something clutch at her heart. 'No, I wouldn't.'

When she came home that evening Hayden's car was not back yet, but Marc was outside playing basketball with

Gregory, the eleven-year-old son of a neighbour. Gregory was tall and gangling, a lonely kid who was left in the care of servants most of the time while his parents travelled around the world.

Marc was wearing a pair of faded denim shorts and a black T-shirt. His arms and legs were deeply tanned and she wondered if in Africa he often wore shorts. The unruly dark hair curled damply around his head. He looked fit and vital and full of energy. She watched his body move as he leaped up, back and legs straight, arm curving to toss the ball through the hoop. Under the dark skin, his muscles moved with sleek, sure precision, and she felt the familiar, treacherous warmth flooding through her body. Taking a deep breath, she got out of the car, hearing Marc's patient voice as he coached the boy. Daniella went into the kitchen to say hello to Mrs Bell and Cora Lee, as she always did when she came home, and they sat around the big kitchen table and had a cup of coffee.

'Julie called,' Mrs Bell said. 'She wants you to call her as soon as you get a chance. I told her it was high time she came up and visited again, but I'm not sure she heard me. She seemed very excited about something for sure.'

The back door opened and Marc and Gregory came in. Marc opened the refrigerator and took out two Cokes. 'Mrs Bell,' he said, 'I'll skip dinner, if you don't mind. Gregory and I will grab a hamburger somewhere and catch a movie.'

'That's fine,' Mrs Bell said. 'No problem. Have fun, you two!' Her voice was warm.

They went back outside, gulping the Coke.

'That boy could use a little grown-up attention,' Mrs Bell said. 'It's nice of Marc to spend some time with him. The kid was here all afternoon, too.'

Daniella drank her coffee. There was still that kind, compassionate side to Marc's character, except he reserved it for others. For her there was only the anger and the contempt. It was a bitter thought.

In her room, Daniella slipped out of her skirt and blouse and put on a kimono. Later she'd get dressed for dinner. She walked into her studio to put away some supplies she'd bought and glanced at the painting she'd been working on the day before. She'd felt good about it yesterday, very good, and she'd wondered if the feeling would hold up under more sober scrutiny. She stood in front of the table, and looked down at the water-colour painting taped to the top. No, she was not unhappy: the colours were good. There was work to be done, certainly, but it was a good beginning.

It smelled stuffy in the studio, and she opened the french doors, finding them unlocked. She frowned. Last night she'd locked the doors and today she hadn't even been in her studio. Nobody ever came in here without her permission and she kept the place clean herself. Well, sort of clean, anyway. She glanced at the dusty shelves and grimaced. She felt vaguely uneasy as she surveyed the room, but there was no sign of any disturbance. She shook away the feeling.

Dusk was settling over the gardens, giving the lush green of the trees and grass a vaguely bluish hue. Daniella took in a deep breath of the fresh air and moved back to her room. She'd better call Julie. She settled herself on the bed and leaned comfortably against the pillows; talking to Julie was always a long affair. She dialled the number and waited. Julie picked up at the first ring, as if she'd been sitting by the phone.

'I've got great news!' Julie's voice practically danced over the wires.

Julie was the only person from her home town with whom Daniella still had contact. She was her best friend from high school. Julie and her family had been one of the few reasons she'd stuck it out as long as she had. She'd spent a lot of time in their noisy, untidy household: five children, a mother who wrote children's books and wasn't too keen on housework, a father who liked to play the comedian, lots of fun and laughter and always an extra plate at the dinner-table for her. Oh, how she had envied Julie her family: the warmth and laughter of a mother and father who loved each other and their children and showed it.

This is what I want later, she'd thought a thousand times, as she'd watched the family around the dinner-table. A husband, children. And I'll do it right; we'll be happy and have fun.

It was what she still wanted—more than anything. More than becoming a famous painter, more than anything money could buy.

She smiled into the telephone. 'You sound as if you're ready to burst, Julie. Tell me the news, quick!'

Julie was married now—to a biology teacher at the local high school, a man who was very popular with both students and parents.

'Oh, Daniella, I can't believe it.' Her voice ran over with happiness. 'I'm pregnant!'

Daniella felt a rush of joy. 'That's wonderful! I'm so happy for you, Julie.'

'You know... it's been more than a year and I... I was beginning to think something was wrong. Oh, Daniella, I was so worried.' There was a catch in Julie's voice, emotion almost getting the better of her.

'You worried too much.'

'I wanted a baby!'

Daniella laughed. 'You're going to have one!'

They talked for another half-hour, catching up on all the news from the family. After she hung up the telephone Daniella closed her eyes, feeling a sudden wave of desolation wash over her. Julie deserved her happiness. She deserved her nice husband, her baby. Why then did it hurt so much to hear her talk about her life? All through her teenage years Daniella had been envious of Julie, and the feeling hadn't gone. It was still there. Why not me? Why can't I have what she has? She didn't like feeling like this. It made her feel so ungrateful for what she already had.

'Oh, come off it,' she told herself out loud, and jumped off the bed. 'You're not even twenty-four years old, not exactly on the shelf yet. Who knows, ten years from now you'll be married with five children! There's time—plenty of time.' But the images that came to mind were those of dark-haired children with earnest grey eyes and they all looked like Marc.

Marc. She remembered well the night she looked into those magnetic grey eyes for the first time—the cold, rainy night Hayden brought her home.

That fateful Sunday night her life changed forever.

CHAPTER FOUR

IT was a cold, blustery Sunday in March when she left Richmond to come to Washington, arriving by bus in the late morning. She headed straight for the Museum of Modern Art and spent hours studying the paintings, captivated and transfixed, not eating, forgetting time.

It was almost closing-time before she realised how late it was, and she left the building to find it dark and raining. Wind lashed at her hair and clothes and she shivered.

She began to walk, still in a daze, her head full of bright images, excitement, hope. Reality caught up with her fast as the rain soaked her jeans and thin jacket. She didn't know where to go; she stopped under a street lamp and got out her map. The YWCA—that was where girls in strange cities went. You could get a room there, cheap—she hoped. She found the location but wasn't sure how far it was and if she could walk it or needed some sort of transport. She folded the map, berating herself for getting caught in the rain, after dark, in a place she didn't know. She was smarter than that; it was stupid, stupid! Washington DC was not the place to be alone at night.

She almost ran back to the museum, back inside where it was warm and dry.

A balding security guard stood near the door, talking to a tall man wearing a Burberry raincoat. He had an impressive head of silver grey hair, immaculately groomed, and he radiated power and sophistication.

'We're closing in fifteen minutes, miss,' the guard said, frowning at her wet, dripping figure.

'I know, I know.' She shivered. 'I need to know how to get to the Y. I mean, is there a bus I can take?'

'The Y?'

'The YWCA. I can get a room there, can't I?'

'I wouldn't know, miss.'

She was suddenly aware of the other man, his brown eyes fixed on her face. There was an odd look in those eyes—pain, sadness, she wasn't sure which. She felt suddenly very self-conscious. 'I'm sorry,' she said, 'I didn't mean to interrupt.'

He waved a hand in dismissal. 'Never mind.' He frowned. 'I wouldn't count on finding a bus. Did you call to find out if you can stay at the Y?'

'No.' She fingered the map nervously, feeling utterly stupid, aware of his eyes looking at her intently, as if searching her face for something.

The guard opened the door and looked outside. 'Mr Penbrooke,' he said, 'your car is here.'

'Thank you.' The man picked up a leather briefcase leaning against the wall. 'Come along,' he said to Daniella, 'I'll give you a ride; this is no time for you to be out by yourself.'

Daniella hesitated—she didn't know this Mr Penbrooke from Adam. She looked at the guard, who gave her a nod of reassurance. 'If you want to be safe, I'd go with him if I were you,' he said.

'Thank you, Tony,' the man said drily. There were laughing lights in the brown eyes and the sadness was gone. Daniella hoisted the duffel-bag on to her shoulder and followed him out of the door into the dark, rainy night. A uniformed chauffeur was holding a large, black umbrella over their heads as they hurried down the steps.

The car was not just a car—it was a black stretch limousine, gleaming in the rain. She'd never ridden in a limousine and as she settled back, enveloped in the comfort of the luxuriously upholstered seat, she felt a sense of unreality take over. For a moment she closed her eyes, praying she wasn't doing a stupid thing getting into this car with a man she didn't know.

'Relax,' the man said and there was humour in his voice. 'I won't bite.'

She couldn't help but smile; being bitten was the least of her worries. He sounded like Santa Claus talking to a frightened little girl.

The car moved noiselessly down the street. Fatigue washed over her. She shivered in her wet clothes and she pushed a damp strand of hair behind her ear, uncomfortably aware of her dishevelled appearance. She looked down at her dirty, worn sneakers. 'I'm making your car all wet.'

'It'll dry.' The brown eyes held hers. 'Did you run away from home?'

She didn't know why the question took her by surprise. 'No,' she said. She hadn't run away from home—she'd left, and that had been almost two years ago. She'd had the good sense to stick it out at her grandfather's house until she'd graduated from high school. She'd also had the good sense to work hard and graduate with honours. She'd had a plan and she needed to be well prepared. Coming to Washington was the next step in her plan.

The man scrutinised her face. 'How old are you?'

'Twenty.'

'You have a driver's licence?'

She sighed. 'Yes.' She fished for it in her canvas bag. He thought she was lying, which was no surprise. Short, blonde and skinny, dressed in jeans and wearing no make-up, she barely looked eighteen. Not that it was any of his business, but she was happy to be out of the weather and if he wanted proof, he could have it.

She produced the licence and gave it to him. He studied it for a moment. 'Daniella——' he said, trying out the sound of it '—a beautiful name.'

'Thank you.' Her mother had not been able to offer her much, but she had given her a beautiful name. Don't let them call you Danny, she'd said a hundred times. After all these years, Daniella could still hear her mother's voice echoing in her mind.

The man handed her back the licence. 'Well,' he said with a doubtful little smile, 'I guess if you want to roam the city-streets on a rainy night, you're allowed to.'

'I don't want to. I was in the museum all afternoon and I forgot the time; when I went out it was dark and raining. I just didn't know. Then I went back in to see if...if I could find out about a bus.'

'What are you doing in the museum?' She stared at him, nonplussed, and he laughed, holding up a hand. 'OK, OK. Silly question.'

Maybe it wasn't so silly, considering her appearance. Her stomach growled inelegantly. 'Sorry,' she muttered.

'Are you hungry?'

'I forgot to eat.'

'You forgot to eat and you forgot the time. It must have been very interesting.'

'It was. The Kelsey exhibition was wonderful, didn't you think so?'

'I didn't see it.' He gave a crooked little smile. 'I was there to see the curator—a friend of mine.'

'Oh, I see. That's too bad. I mean it's too bad you didn't see the exhibition! She's so good.'

'Who's Kelsey?'

'She does water-colours and pastels. She's famous.'
She sighed. 'I wish I were half as good.'

'You paint?'

'Water-colours, yes. I like using ink and charcoal and
pastels with them, too. I want to go to art school, but
first I'll have to find a job and a place to stay. I want
to be ready to start in September.'

'So that's why you've come to Washington?'

'Yes. The museums are here, the galleries. Maybe New
York is better, but...' she shrugged '...it's farther and
bigger. I'll try Washington first.'

The man smiled at her, humour in his eyes. Oh, God,
she thought, he thinks I'm nuts. He thinks I don't know
what I'm talking about.

Then he leaned forward and spoke to the driver—she
couldn't hear the words. She felt a pang of fear. What
if he kidnapped her? She glanced out of the window,
seeing lights flash by. A big road, trees. She had no idea
where she was.

'Where are we?' She shivered uncontrollably.

'The Parkway.'

'Is that where the YWCA is?'

He smiled. 'No. You're coming home with me. What
you need is a hot meal and a good night's sleep; you
look fit to drop.'

She was tired, but not stupid. She shook her head.
'No. Please just take me to the YWCA.' Her hands began
to tremble and she clasped them in her lap. 'Or I'll get
out here, if that's easier.' First you must stay calm.

He laughed again. 'You don't want to be stranded
here.' His eyes reflected his laugh, and a twinge of
concern. 'Don't worry, you're quite safe.'

She swallowed hard. 'How do I know that's true?'

He smiled. 'Well, I guess you'll have to take Tony's
word for it.'

'I don't know Tony; I don't know you.'

He gave a low laugh. 'Maybe I can help you out here.' He picked up a leather briefcase, lifted it on to his knees and opened it. It contained a lap-top computer, papers and files. He fished out a magazine and handed it over. *Business Week*, she read.

'Page thirty-two.'

She found the page and skimmed the words—something about a merger. A picture in the top left corner showed two men shaking hands. One of them was the man sitting right next to her. 'Hayden Penbrooke (left) and Conrad Harrington (right) shaking hands on a deal that took six months to complete', the caption read. The magazine was taken out of her hands before she had much more than a glimpse, but it was enough to know that Hayden Penbrooke was a man of money and influence and apparently a well-known figure in the business community.

'Relax,' he said again.

She didn't know what to say or what to do—it was a strange situation. Why had a man like Hayden Penbrooke offered to give her a lift? Why was he now taking her home with him? She scrutinised his face: it was strong-featured and mildly arrogant, yet the brown eyes were friendly and amused. She didn't feel threatened, just flabbergasted. 'Why are you doing this?' she asked.

He shrugged, giving a crooked smile. 'I have no idea.' But there was something in his eyes, a touch of sadness, and she knew instinctively that there was a special reason why he had offered her a ride and why he was now taking her to his house.

The Penbrooke house was not a house—it was more like a mansion, that much she could see, even in the dark. She was ushered into the large kitchen and a woman appeared magically and in a short time produced a hot roast beef sandwich with thick, rich gravy and a glass of milk.

Hayden sat down too and was given a cup of coffee. He was talking to the woman—a Mrs Bell—but Daniella was too tired and too hungry to pay attention. She ate the food eagerly, trying not to appear too much like a starving dog attacking a bone.

Mrs Bell was shaking her head. 'Child, what was you doing out on your own on a night like this?'

'I just got into town,' Daniella said. 'I was looking for the YWCA.'

'Don't you have no friends here?'

Daniella shook her head. She was beginning to feel like a helpless little girl who was being chided for being reckless and irresponsible. Well, she had been, hadn't she?

The door opened and a man entered. He was tall and well-built with dark hair and the lightest eyes she had ever seen. 'I smell coffee...' he said '...I was hoping...' His eyes met hers and he stopped in mid-sentence. Daniella's heart lurched—she didn't know why. His eyes made her grow warm all over.

She swallowed her food, lowering her gaze to her plate, barely hearing Hayden Penbrooke making introductions. Marc was his name—Marc Penbrooke, the son. She mumbled an acknowledgement, feeling painfully aware of her bedraggled appearance, her damp hair.

Mrs Bell poured another cup of coffee and Marc sat down at the table as well. 'So, you just arrived in town today?' he asked. She said yes, and told him what she had told his father: about wanting to go to art school and wanting to find a job—all the while aware of the penetrating grey eyes never leaving her face. He told her he'd spent the last year in Peru, South America and he was now getting ready to go to Africa for three years to work on a rural water project in Ghana. He was leaving in a month.

One month—not a long time, but long enough to fall hopelessly, helplessly in love.

On Thursday her three days to consider the quarter-million-dollar proposal were up. She had briefly seen Marc at breakfast and not again for the rest of the day. Only Hayden was in the dining-room when she arrived for their customary pre-dinner drink. She hoped Marc was out and wouldn't show up, but she had no such luck. He came in ten minutes later, wearing a suit and tie, looking cool and collected. He'd probably been to the District for contract negotiations. He'd even had his hair cut. In his business clothes he looked more polished, and devastatingly attractive; just looking at him made her heart beat in a frantic rhythm. It made her angry with herself; she didn't want to feel this way every time she saw him. She didn't want him to have so much power over her feelings. His eyes met hers and she felt the tension quivering in the air around her.

She took a deep breath. 'What a gorgeous day!' she said cheerfully, determined not to show him her uneasy emotions. 'Did you see the azaleas? And the red tulips?'

They had.

'I was right about the red tulips, wasn't I?' she went on, smiling at Hayden. 'I knew they'd be gorgeous in that corner by those rocks. We should get more. Loads of them. Shall I ask Ben to get more this autumn?'

Wrong, wrong. She realised her mistake as soon as she saw Marc's face; his eyes were throwing daggers at her. Her words had not been those of a person preparing for departure with a quarter of a million dollars in her pocket. Next year's tulips would probably not feature high on her list of priorities in such a situation.

Hayden's face was a more comforting sight—he was smiling at her, his brown eyes amused. He always enjoyed her enthusiasm. 'Yes, yes, you were right, and by all means let Ben get some more. Just don't step on his professional toes with your artistic interpretations.' He handed her a glass of wine.

'Of course not. I'll make him think it was his idea in the first place!'

Hayden threw back his head and laughed. 'You should be in business, or politics.'

'A very liberated idea, Hayden, considering I'm of the female persuasion—you're learning.'

He put an arm around her and drew her to his side. 'How can I not, with you around to corrupt my principles and opinions?'

Not to speak of your morals, she thought, slanting a glance at Marc, who stood, silent and glowering, by the bar.

During dinner she managed to keep the conversation light, well aware that Marc was not making much of a contribution. Afterwards they retired to the library, where she and Hayden often spent the evenings reading, watching TV or playing chess. Hayden had taught her to play the game and she'd learned quickly, much to her own surprise. In her previous life—as she called her life before she'd met Hayden—it had never occurred to her that one day she would play chess. The game of the day then had been dodging her grandfather's rages.

Cora Lee brought them coffee on a tea-trolley and Daniella said she'd pour it.

'Black for you, Marc?'

'Please.' He was reading the newspaper and she couldn't see his face. She didn't want to, either. She put his coffee-cup on the small table by his side, then poured some for herself and Hayden.

'Thank you. How about some chess?' he asked. 'Or would you rather do something else?'

'Chess is fine.' It would demand all her concentration and divert her thoughts.

And it did. It was a long game. She became aware at some point that Marc was following the moves, but she was able, by some miracle, to block him out. In the end she lost, but only barely.

'Heck,' she said to Hayden, smiling. 'I thought I had you there.'

Hayden laughed. 'So did I.' He got to his feet. 'I'm off to bed.' He leaned towards her and kissed her on the forehead. 'Goodnight.'

She got up as well. 'I'd better go up too.'

'I need to talk to you,' Marc said. 'It'll only take a moment.'

'Play her a game of chess,' Hayden suggested. 'I'll guarantee you she'll win.'

Daniella bit her lip.

'Another time, maybe,' Marc said blandly.

Hayden opened the door. 'Well, goodnight then.' He went out and closed the door behind him. Daniella remained standing, regarding Marc in silence.

'You're very good, aren't you?' he asked.

She was puzzled. 'Oh?'

'At chess. Strategy, thinking ahead.'

She nodded solemnly. 'It's a gift.'

His mouth twisted. 'Used to your every advantage.'

'Of course.' She smiled. 'Isn't that the smart thing to do in this life?'

He didn't answer. He scrutinised her for a long, tense moment, his eyes coolly contemptuous.

'Your time is up,' he said, breaking the silence.

CHAPTER FIVE

SHE frowned. 'My time is up? Oh . . . you mean the three days I had to consider your proposal?'

'Right.' He got to his feet and put his hands in his pockets, observing her coolly. 'So you like red tulips?'

Red tulips? It took her less than a moment to catch on. 'Yes.' She smiled brightly. 'Don't you?'

He ignored her question. 'Smart move at dinner—mentioning the tulips. Trying to needle me a little?'

'Actually, no. It was quite spontaneous.'

His eyes narrowed. 'Does that mean you're not accepting my offer?' He moved towards her, towering over her.

She anchored her feet to the floor and stared at him stonily. 'That's right.'

His face went rigid with anger, the square jaw rock-hard. 'A quarter of a million is not enough, is it?'

'No.' No money could buy what she would have to give up; no money was worth it. It hadn't taken her three days to figure it out—she'd known it long ago.

He grabbed her shoulders. 'You think you can get more? I warned you it was my final offer.'

'I'm quite aware of it.'

'What do you want?'

She met his gaze. 'I want to stay here.'

He released his hold on her shoulders and shoved her away from him. 'Everybody has her price. Especially people like you!'

She smiled at him sweetly. 'Find mine. By my guest.'

Without another word, he turned on his heel and marched out of the room.

She wondered why he cared so much. If he was worried about his father's money, why wasn't he here taking care of it? He was preparing to leave again, to live thousands of miles away in a poor country, eating simple food, living a difficult, rugged life.

Something was wrong. Something simply didn't make sense.

Andrew came to see her paintings the next day and they managed to come to a satisfactory decision concerning the selection for the group show. Andrew was a handsome man with impeccably styled dark hair and seductive deep blue eyes. He loved his art gallery, his women and his food. Despite the fact that he was an incorrigible womaniser, she liked him, his easy-going nature and generosity. When she'd first started working for him she'd known nothing, but he had helped and advised her and encouraged her with her painting. 'You've got talent and vision,' he'd said, 'and a lovely feel for colour, but what you need is technique.'

She'd started classes at the Corcoran School of Art with the help of a scholarship and a loan from Hayden. He'd offered to pay her way—everything—but she had refused and stood her ground. She had, however, accepted his offer to live at the house. So had begun the happiest time in her life.

And now there was a show at the Benedict.

'There's nothing to be nervous about,' Andrew said. 'We're doing a lot of advertising. You'll do fine.' He drew her into his arms and kissed her gently. For a moment she leaned against him. Everything would be so much easier if she could just love Andrew. But she didn't. And she'd known it for quite some time, but for some reason it was more clear to her now than it had been before.

No, not just *some* reason.

A very particular reason: Marc.

She sighed and Andrew released her. 'You're no fun.'

She feigned confusion. 'What do you want?' She knew very well what he wanted—he'd wanted it for three years.

'Passionate love, right here in your studio.'

'The floor is too hard.'

He scowled at her. 'As I said, you're no fun.'

She gave him a half-smile. 'I'm sorry.'

'No, you're not. You know what you need?'

She looked him square in the face. 'Yes. A wild and passionate love affair.'

He spread out his arms. 'I'm available.'

'But I'm not passionately in love with you.'

He put his hand over his heart in a gesture of sincerity. 'Give me a chance. Let me show you my true passionate self.'

She laughed. He'd been saying that for three years, and in between the various occasions he'd divorced his wife and had affairs with other women—women who were less resistant than her. Daniella wondered why he kept coming back. Probably simply for the challenge. He was incapable of admitting defeat.

'Let's go away for the weekend,' Andrew suggested. 'A long weekend in some cosy country inn. I know just the place in West Virginia. Very romantic, very idyllic.' He smiled suggestively. 'You'll love it.'

She stacked some paintings against the wall. 'Stop it, Andrew.'

He put his arm around her shoulder and put his mouth against her ear. 'Are you afraid,' he whispered, 'that I'll awaken desires and passions in you you won't know what to do with?'

'No,' she said calmly, twisting away from him. 'Out of my way, paintings coming through.'

He let out a long-suffering sigh. 'At least come to the party with me tonight—we'll have dinner first.'

'What party?'

He waved his hand. 'A friend's.'

Andrew had more friends than he knew what to do with, which was part of the reason he was now divorced. His wife had not wanted to share him quite as extensively with friends and other hangers on. She wanted him home, in front of the fire with his newspaper, once in a while. Andrew wanted to party, all the time.

She shook her head. 'I don't feel like going to a party. People drink too much, they gossip too much. Some photographer will know who I am and wonder what I'm doing there with you.'

'No photographers.'

She hesitated. Hayden was in New York and wouldn't be home until tomorrow and being home alone with Marc would not be an uplifting experience.

Andrew put a hand on her shoulder. 'Daniella,' he said, insistence in his voice, 'it will be good PR.'

'PR for what?'

He sighed impatiently. 'For the show, Daniella, the show. There will be some interesting people there, people with money. People with free time to hang around at art galleries, specifically the Benedict if we play it right.'

'OK, OK,' she relented.

'Good. And remember now, advertise yourself a little. Make sure you bring up the show whenever you can, but for God's sake, don't bore them.'

Daniella grimaced. 'I like painting. I don't like selling myself.'

Andrew groaned. 'Oh, God, the artistic sensibilities! Just stay close to me and for heaven's sake go put on something else.'

She glanced down at her jeans and T-shirt. 'All right, why not? I'll put on my leopard-skin dress, the one with the slit up to here.' She traced her finger up her thigh to her hip. 'They'll all notice me then.'

For a moment alarm flared in his eyes and she laughed out loud. He jumped up, took her hand and dragged her into her bedroom. He opened the wardrobe doors. 'All right, let's see what you have in here.'

'Hey, wait a minute, mister!'

He didn't answer. He riffled through the coat-hangers, making faces as he examined her clothes.

'I can dress myself!' she said angrily, sounding like a child.

'I hope so,' he muttered. He took out a white dress and tossed it on the bed, a black one followed, then the silk one she'd had on the night Marc had come home. 'Try these. I want to see them.'

'I'll wear the black one.' She held it up in front of her. 'It's elegantly sexy.'

'I want to see all three.'

She glared at him. 'No! I'll be damned if I have you decide what I'll wear tonight!'

'Daniella!' he bellowed. 'You want people to come and see your show?'

'Yes, but——'

A hard knocking on the door interrupted her. Clutching the black dress to her chest she went to open it.

Marc stood in the door, his face a mask of granite, his wintry eyes sweeping across the room taking in Andrew sitting on the edge of the bed, tie loosened, the dresses on the bed. His gaze moved back to her, settling on her face with icy contempt.

Daniella felt her heart sink into her shoes. A shiver went down her spine at the expression in his eyes. Then she rallied her defences and straightened her spine. This was utterly stupid. She was not going to be intimidated by his idiotic suspicions.

'Let me introduce you. Marc...'

Andrew jumped up from the bed, hand stretched out, smiling. 'Marc Penbrooke? I'm Andrew Benedict. Good to meet you.'

Marc shook his hand and gave him a cold nod of his head, saying nothing. He glanced back at Daniella.

'Mrs Bell wants to know if you'll be here for dinner.'

She looked right into his eyes. Damn him for his arrogance, his judgemental attitude. 'No, I won't. I was just about to let her know. Andrew and I are going out.'

He nodded. 'I see.' The words dropped like chips of ice.

Oh, no, you don't, she said silently. You're blind and deaf.

He turned on his heel and strode out, closing the door behind him.

Andrew raised a quizzical brow. 'What's with him?'

Daniella shrugged carelessly. 'Who knows? Why don't you go have a drink with him and find out while I get dressed?'

'You're so generous,' he said drily. He moved towards the studio door. 'I'll wait here. Your paintings are better company. Try the white dress first.'

'I'm wearing the black one, *finito*.' She gave him a little shove and closed the door behind him.

She enjoyed the party more than she had expected, and Andrew didn't let an opportunity slip by to casually mention the fact that the Benedict was having a group show next month and Daniella was one of the exhibiting artists. He stirred up quite a lot of interest and Daniella answered questions and talked about her painting, feeling quite the celebrity on her own merit. She was used to getting attention whenever she attended a party or reception with Hayden, but this was different. This had nothing to do with Hayden; this was because of her own work. It felt good.

It was well past one o'clock when Andrew dropped her off at the house. He kissed her goodnight. 'You were great,' he said.

She laughed. 'You mean you were. Your bragging was indecent!'

'It's called advertising; besides, you lapped up all the attention.'

She made a face at him. 'Goodnight, Andrew.'

She moved quietly through the hall, noticing the light from the half-open door of the library. Hayden was in New York, so it was Marc who was still up. The next moment the door swung open further and Marc loomed in the doorway.

'You're back,' he stated. 'Did you have a good time?' His gaze swept over her in cool appraisal.

'Very, thank you.' She felt naked in the short dress, but was determined not to be intimidated.

'Is this a habit of yours, going out with men when my father is out of sight?'

'I'm not sure what you mean,' she said calmly.

'Maybe he's a little old for you,' he said in a slow, patient tone as if he were explaining something to a dull child. 'Maybe he can't quite satisfy your youthful appetites, so you have your little escapades on the side when he's not looking.'

She didn't know whether to laugh or get mad. 'I don't know why you should object,' she said lightly, falling easily back into her act. 'Hayden doesn't. He thinks I should go out with people my own age and have some fun.' Good lord, she thought, where is this going to end?

'Men?'

'Why not?'

'You're despicable,' he said with quiet rage.

She shrugged. 'Hayden doesn't think so.'

'I'll bet he doesn't know half of what you're up to.'

She raised her brows in question. 'Like what?'

'Like tonight. Did he know you were going out with that dry-cleaned yuppie philanderer until all hours of the night?'

'As a matter of fact, he didn't, no. It came up at the last minute.'

'I'll bet. Pretty smart, aren't you?'

She sighed. 'If all this gives you so much trouble, Marc, by all means discuss it with your father. Maybe he'll see it your way and tell me to leave.'

His eyes narrowed dangerously. 'You're pretty sure of yourself, aren't you?'

She smiled brightly. 'Very.'

'It's not prudent to be too sure,' he said coldly. 'What if, just for the sake of argument, he tells you to leave?'

She held his gaze, not wavering. 'Then I'll leave,' she said calmly.

'Just like that.'

'Just like that. I won't have a choice, will I?'

'You have a choice now.'

She shook her head. 'You don't understand.' Marc knew the story of her arrival but he did not know why she was still there, three years later. At least, he didn't know the *real* story. The real story only a few people knew. It was the gossip printed in the papers and doing the rounds at cocktail parties that everyone was familiar with. It was that story Marc knew and believed. And that was why he now wanted her out of his father's house. But she wasn't going—not until Hayden himself told her to leave.

'Oh, I understand all right,' he said scornfully.

Anger mixed with pain. She wished it didn't hurt, but it did. His face was an impenetrable mask, his jaw rigid, his eyes cold. He wouldn't believe her, no matter what she said, yet somewhere in her head a voice kept jabbing at her. Tell him, tell him! She did not want to defend herself against malicious gossip, yet she wanted to tell him the truth once, only once. Then he could never accuse her of not telling him, of hiding the truth.

'I know all the things you're thinking,' she said calmly, looking into the scornful eyes. 'But you're wrong: I'm not your father's mistress.'

His laugh was hard and sarcastic. 'Running scared?'

She shook her head. 'No.'

'I'm not stupid, sweetheart.' He straightened, filling the doorway with his bulk. 'Don't make a mistake about it.'

'What's the matter with you?' Anne asked, frowning.

They were examining paint charts since the artist whose exhibit would follow the Keiler show had demanded a pale silvery grey as a backdrop for his paintings. Painting walls wasn't one of Daniella's favourite activities, but it came with the territory. At present the walls were stark white. Daniella examined the varieties of grey, trying to find one to match the sample the artist had sent them.

'What do you mean, what's the matter with me? Nothing is the matter with me.'

'You're distracted, you don't hear half of what I say, you're irritable and jittery. Are you nervous about your show? It's still weeks away.'

'No...oh, I don't know...maybe.'

Anne scrutinised her face. 'It's Marc, isn't it?'

Daniella sighed. 'He's getting on my nerves.'

She wasn't even sure why. Everything had been more or less normal for the past week or so. 'Normal' meaning he'd not said anything hostile or sarcastic to her. At mealtimes the three of them would engage in conversation that seemed quite relaxed—as long as the topics were neutral. Marc had taken Gregory out fishing a couple of mornings, so they discussed fish and water pollution. A friend of Hayden's was selling his villa near Athens and Hayden considered buying it. They discussed Greece and tourism.

However, whenever Hayden's business affairs or Marc's career entered the conversation, tempers flared. Although the feelings were never expressed in words, Daniella was quite aware of them. Hayden felt abandoned by his son, who was not living up to his obligations. Marc felt his father was a single-minded despot who wanted to control him and he had no intention of giving in. Both of them felt misunderstood. At times, the tension between father and son was so intense that Daniella had the urge to flee from the room. Instead, she tried to keep the peace by whatever means she was able to, usually by humour or a change of topic.

She wondered to what extent her presence in the household was responsible for Marc's anger with his father. Quite some, she supposed. It was not a happy thought. Blindly, she stared at the paint charts, wondering what Marc was up to. Certainly he had not yet given up trying to get her out of his father's house, had he? She wondered what game he was playing. Maybe none. Maybe he had just given up. Fat chance, she told herself. He made her nerves frayed. She felt as if there were something hanging over her head, something elusive she couldn't see or touch.

'Jade's party will do you good,' Anne said. 'Let the psychic tell you your fortune—maybe that'll cheer you up.'

Daniella grimaced. 'Or depress me even more. Besides, I'm not having anybody tell me my fortune.'

'Why not?'

'Psychics scare me.'

Anne laughed. 'Why?'

'Because they may be right. Maybe I don't want to know what's going to happen.'

'You don't have to believe it; it's all just in fun.'

Daniella bit her lip. 'I'm not so sure, I think there are some who are for real, and they know what they're doing.'

'Well, I'll check with Jade later and make sure she got a fake one!'

Despite herself, Daniella laughed. 'Oh, Anne, be quiet.'

Daniella was in her room, dressing for the party. She had to admit she was looking forward to it. Jade Devereaux believed in fun, and she was one of the few people in the Washington high society set who seemed to be genuinely herself and not care one hoot about what anyone said about her or her husband. Being independently wealthy, and lacking all political ambition, she could afford not to care.

'I've seen and done it all, love,' she'd said to Daniella, 'and believe me, it's not worth it. Life's too short.' She'd come to this conclusion at the ripe old age of twenty-nine, having spent her life in Hong Kong where her

English father and Chinese mother had lived the high society life in the upper levels of the world of business and politics. Now, married to an American newspaper reporter, she was letting her hair down and having the time of her life.

Daniella zipped up her dress and surveyed her reflection in the mirror, smiling at herself. The flirty little dress of jade-green silk organza fitted her mood perfectly. When she went out with Hayden she usually dressed a little more conservatively, but tonight she wanted to have just plain fun. She put the finishing touches to her make-up and slipped into her high-heeled shoes. With a last glance in the mirror, she picked up her evening bag and went downstairs to the library. Hayden was sitting in his chair, coffee at his elbow, reading the paper. Marc was not there. Earlier in the day she'd seen him in the kitchen with Gregory, working on some strange contraption which apparently was Gregory's science project for school. They'd been so engrossed, they hadn't even noticed her as she poured herself a cup of coffee.

Hayden looked up from his paper and smiled. 'You look ravishing,' he said.

She performed a little curtsy. 'Why, thank you, sir.' She touched his shoulder. 'Are you sure you don't want to come?'

'Very sure. I'm getting too old for this sort of thing.'

'You're not old.' She didn't like him talking like that; she didn't want to think of him as getting older. She wanted him the way he was for ever.

'Of course not,' he said. 'I'm only old when I don't want to do something.'

She laughed and kissed him on the cheek. 'I should have known. You're so smart.'

He patted her hand, smiling. 'Go, have fun.'

She arrived at the party, spotting Anne on the other side of the room, dressed in a voluminous black dress gathered around her waist with a multicoloured fringed scarf. Around her neck she had draped an exotic collection of strange beads and stones and wood, and her hair stood out like a dark red halo. She was holding a glass of wine in her hand and seemed amicably in discussion with a short, balding man wearing thick glasses.

When Daniella approached them, Anne grabbed her hand. 'Daniella, I want you to meet Jeremy. He's just come back from Tibet. He lived with the monks there for a year, can you believe it? He says it really opened him up and has done a lot for his creativity. He's a painter. I'd love to see his work, wouldn't you?'

Daniella smiled at the man and extended her hand. 'Hi, I'm Daniella Michaels.'

'Oh, sorry,' Anne said. 'I forgot to introduce you. She's a painter too, Jeremy, and my friend. Her work will be in a group show at the Benedict next month.'

They talked about painting and Tibet and monks and the purity of the soul. They had something to eat and something to drink. In the next room, the floor was cleared and people began to dance to the music. Daniella mingled and talked and danced and enjoyed herself. She had not yet seen anything of the psychic, which was fine by her.

After a while she went back for a glass of mineral water and a friend pulled her down on the couch. 'Tell me about your show. Do I get an invitation?'

Other women were sitting around, sipping drinks and apparently discussing the love-life of one of them.

'I never understood why you dropped him,' one of them said.

The tall, beautiful one waved her hand in dismissal. Diamonds sparkled and glittered. 'It was years ago.' She wore a daring cobalt-blue dress. Daring, but gorgeous, Daniella decided. With a very expensive label on the inside, no doubt.

'But why? What was the big secret?'

Daniella studied the woman. She was striking, with large, dark eyes, high cheekbones and lustrous black hair. Yet the corners of her mouth turned down slightly and she had a vaguely petulant look about her. The woman shrugged. 'He deceived me. He misrepresented himself. I had certain...expectations and he chose not to fulfil them.'

'Oh, come on, Clarissa, you're so diplomatic. Give us the scoop in plain English, will you?'

Clarissa. Daniella frowned. The name echoed in her mind, ringing with a familiarity she couldn't place.

There was laughter all around. The woman called Clarissa smiled. 'Just think——' she said meaningfully '—just think for a moment where I would have been these last four or five years if I'd married him.'

'I thought he left the country because you'd dropped him...wounded pride and all that?'

'No.' Clarissa hesitated, but it was only for show, Daniella could tell: she was lapping up all the attention.

'He'd been at odds with his father,' Clarissa went on. 'Apparently it had been building for years, but I wasn't aware of it. The old man expected him to join the company and, quite frankly, that's what I expected as well.'

Daniella grew still; her breath caught in her throat. They were talking about Marc, no doubt about it. She knew now why the woman's name sounded familiar: Clarissa was the woman Marc had told her about, the woman he had shared his life with for more than two years.

When he had told her about Clarissa their relationship had been over for more than a year and, from his manner, Daniella had surmised that he was no longer broken-hearted but rather considered himself lucky to have escaped the certainty of a miserable marriage. He had not gone into details about what had happened, and she had not felt it was right to ask.

Words, a phrase came back to her now. 'I simply can't understand how I could have been so wrong about a person.' Marc's words, echoing in her memory.

Clarissa lifted her elegant hand and gently rearranged a lock of her dark hair. 'He wanted me to go with him,' she went on. 'He expected me to just pack up and follow him to some wretched jungle village in South America. Peru, I think it was. Can you imagine that?' She shivered, the horror of the idea alone too much to contemplate. 'And think of where he's been the last few years. *Africa!*' She sighed. 'Well, it just wasn't my scene. I had no choice but to...break...it...off.' Her voice trailed oddly and her face turned ghostly white. A deadly silence fell over the group and all eyes stared in the same direction.

Daniella glanced up and felt a sickening lurch of her heart. Marc was standing next to her.

What was he doing here? He seemed unperturbed by the awkward silence, his eyes fixed on the dark-haired woman with calm indifference. For an endless moment they gazed at each other in silence, the centre of everyone's rapt attention.

'Hello, Clarissa,' he said, his voice coolly polite.

Clarissa swallowed visibly, but was apparently unable to return the greeting. Marc looked away, settling his gaze on Daniella. He took her hand and pulled her out of her seat. 'Let's dance,' he said. It sounded like an order, but for some reason she didn't have it in her to protest and she moved with him into the dance room. He swung her into his arms and her body went rigid. 'Relax,' he said.

'Sure, easy,' she said coolly. 'I'm always relaxed when I dance with people who despise me! What are you doing here, anyway?'

'I was invited.' His breath fanned her cheek.

'I see.' It was impossible to relax: her body, so close to his, was beyond her control. She felt the warmth of his skin through the thin fabric of his shirt. She smelled his aftershave—the same familiar scent he had worn three years ago.

'She didn't seem overly delighted to see you,' she said for something to say.

'Do you know Clarissa?'

'No. I'd never met her before today, but I believe you mentioned her once. Something about a rather disastrous love-affair.'

His mouth turned down. 'I have the unfortunate habit of falling for the wrong type.'

'And what type is that?'

'Fortune-hunters, parasites.'

She felt her temperature rise alarmingly, but managed to keep herself under control. 'It must be very difficult,' she said pseudo-sympathetic. 'The trials and tribulations of being wealthy. My heart bleeds for you.'

He gave her a mocking little smile. 'We're good at this, aren't we? Throwing insults at each other.'

'You started it, if I remember correctly. I don't believe in sitting back and docilely taking what is dished out to me. I've had enough stuff I didn't want dished out to me.' She stopped in the middle of the floor and pulled away from him. She didn't care who saw or heard. 'Go find yourself somebody else to insult.' With that she swung out of the room.

She found the bathroom and locked the door. In the mirror her face was flushed, her eyes a deep glittering blue. She sighed and ran cold water over her hands. She should have known that the last week or so had been the silence before the storm; she could quite clearly see the clouds gathering in the sky.

Leaving the bathroom, she ran into Jade.

'Come with me,' she said. 'I want you to meet someone.' Daniella followed Jade out on to the wooden veranda that stretched along the back of the house. The air was fresh and fragrant and cool against her hot cheeks. Only a few people were out—most of them were inside, dancing.

'Simone? I want you to meet my friend Daniella.'

A young woman turned to Daniella. She was small and delicate, with soft brown hair and green eyes. Her face was oddly vulnerable with a sensitive mouth and pale cheeks and in the white dress she seemed almost angelic. 'Hi.' She took both Daniella's hands and smiled. Almost instantly the smile faded and she dropped Daniella's hand as if she'd burned herself. 'I'm sorry,' she muttered, and shook her small hands as if they were wet and she was shaking off the water.

Daniella stared at her, not understanding what was going on.

Jade frowned. 'What's wrong, Simone?'

'Tension.' She smiled apologetically at Daniella. 'There's so much tension in you I could feel it in my hands. I'm sorry.'

Jade scrutinised Daniella's face. 'Problems? Or shouldn't I ask?'

Daniella shrugged, feeling apprehensive. There was no doubt as to the identity of the young woman in the white dress: she was the psychic. Daniella waved her hand. 'Oh, I had a little argument with Marc,' she said lightly, as if it was of no consequence. She was uncomfortably aware of the green eyes watching her closely.

'You're in love with him,' Simone said softly.

Daniella laughed—she couldn't help it. 'I thought I was, once, ages ago.'

'You still are. I think that's where the tension comes in. You're going to have a difficult time, but it will be all right, you know, in the end.' She smiled. 'Sorry, you didn't ask me to tell you this.'

Daniella smiled back. 'It's all right.' She didn't believe anything the woman said anyway. If she could only get away now, without being rude.

'Fascinating,' Jade said. 'You and Marc—it would just be perfect.'

'Oh, for heaven's sake, Jade, don't start anything.'

Jade laughed and turned to Simone. 'What else do you see for her? Something uplifting?'

There was hesitation in the green eyes. Simone shook her head. 'I'm sorry, I shouldn't have said anything in the first place.'

'But you see something else, don't you? Daniella, tell her she can say it.'

Daniella shrugged. 'As long as it isn't bad news.'

'You'll be going on a trip.' Simone closed her eyes in concentration. 'It's very far. Some other continent. I can't tell.'

Jade grinned. 'How about that! A trip. Maybe Hayden will take you on a business trip to some exotic place.'

Simone shook her head. 'You'll be going alone.'

That night Daniella dreamed of Marc again: they were dancing, alone, barefoot in the grass. It was a balmy night full of sweet scents and mystery. A full moon silvered the trees and grass and soft music floated on the air. She leaned against him, feeling so safe, so loved in his embrace, so full of restless longing.

He laid her down on the grass under the willow tree, near the babbling brook at the end of the gardens. He made love to her, his hands and mouth making magic. She smelled the scent of crushed grass and felt the velvet touch of the warm breeze on her skin. Over his shoulder she looked up into the starry sky, knowing she was in heaven.

She awoke, sitting up in bed, crying.

She'd fallen in love with him the moment she had seen him in his father's kitchen, and in the weeks that followed her feelings had grown more intense. She'd never felt anything for a man that could compare to what she was feeling for Marc: it had overwhelmed her completely. He'd been overwhelmed as easily as she had, yet for a while he'd been able to keep his emotions in check, until one night, two days before he'd left.

They'd made love—she'd wanted to desperately and all her common sense had not been able to save her. It had been the most magic, wonderful night of her life; she'd never experienced such love and joy and utter happiness.

Marc had regretted it bitterly afterwards—not the loving, he said, but that he had broken the silent promise he had made to himself and to her not to start something that could not be finished.

'But it doesn't have to end,' she said, fearful, indignant, hurt by his remorse.

'You know it has to, Daniella.' He stroked her hair.

'Why?' She was rebellious, frightened. How could she give him up now? How could he let her go?

'You know why. I'll be in Ghana for the next three years; you'll be here, going to art school, becoming a great painter.' He smiled.

'I'll come with you to Africa,' she said. 'I can paint anywhere.' But it was naïve and impulsive to suggest it and she knew it as soon as she uttered the words.

'No, Daniella. You need to be here, going to school. You have to work on your painting. You have to be here where everything is that you need: the people, the school, the galleries and museums. I would never forgive myself if you gave up what you've always wanted to do.'

She knew he was right, of course. 'So what do we do?' she asked, already knowing the answer, already feeling the pain.

He took her into his arms, holding her very close. 'We'll each do what we must do.'

'And what about us?' She heard the tears in her voice, felt them burning behind her eyes.

'For now we'll have to leave it to fate.'

'Maybe...'

'Ssh...' He silenced her with a kiss. 'No promises. You're only twenty years old, Daniella. You need to be free to find your way. I'm sorry...' His voice was oddly husky. 'I'm not sorry about these last few weeks, I'm just sorry the timing is so bad and that it can't end in a better way.'

She knew the truth of what he said, even if everything inside her rebelled against it.

Maybe he'll write, she thought. Maybe he'll come home for Christmas. But she was too proud to ask. She'd never asked anybody for anything.

But he had not written and he had not come home for Christmas, not the first year nor the two that followed.

Now, after three years, he was back and nothing was as it had been before. The dream had turned into a nightmare.

For the next few days she kept thinking about Clarissa and it angered her. She wondered why her thoughts kept drifting back to the woman and the words she had said, the words Marc had said. Marc had called her a fortune-hunter and a parasite.

Clarissa had dumped him because she hadn't wanted to go to South America with him. Clarissa had not wanted him; she'd wanted the money and prestige that came with being part of the wealthy and influential Penbrooke family. Daniella couldn't blame him for calling *her* a fortune-hunter, not one bit. What hurt was that he felt *she* belonged in the same category.

By all appearances, maybe it looked that way, but it wasn't true. She'd never intended taking advantage of Hayden, if such a thing were possible. She had never intended living in his house, but Hayden himself had asked her to stay. Initially he'd invited her to stay until she'd found a place of her own. When she had, he'd insisted on seeing it. He didn't approve. She found another one. He didn't approve.

'You're never going to approve of any of the places I'm going to find, are you?' she'd asked, fully aware that she didn't need his approval at all.

He'd given her a crooked little smile. 'I don't want you to leave: I like having you here.'

He had all the right reasons and in the end he had managed, despite her pride and sense of independence, to persuade her to stay. She'd asked him why he had taken her home that rainy night in March and again she'd seen that odd glimpse of sadness in his eyes.

'Because you reminded me of my daughter,' he'd said, giving a half-smile. 'Or, at least, what I thought she might have looked like if she'd grown to be your age. She was a skinny little thing, like you. You stood there with that map in your hand, looking lost. For a moment I wondered how I would feel if my daughter stood there, soaked to the skin, not knowing where to go. You got in the car and I looked at you, at those big blue eyes of yours, thinking you were someone's daughter. Someone who might be very worried about you.'

'Nobody was worried about me.'

'That was even worse.' His mouth quirked, as if mocking his own sentimentality. 'And then you started talking about your painting and I saw the shine in your eyes, yet you looked so cold and bedraggled. How could I not take you home with me?'

She'd been with Hayden for three years now and she loved him for his kindness and caring. She only wished Marc could see how it really was between them. But maybe it was impossible for him to believe that she was any better than Clarissa. Maybe his experience had blinded him to the truth.

At lunchtime the following Tuesday, Marc appeared in the gallery. Daniella noticed him as her heart gave a crazy leap and she lowered her gaze to the counter, pretending she wasn't aware of him. He'd not been here before and she was surprised to see him. There were a number of visitors and for a few moments he simply wandered around, studying the paintings like the rest of them.

'What's wrong?' Anne asked.

'Marc's here.'

Anne had not been introduced to Marc, but she'd seen him at Jade's party. 'Marc?' Anne's gaze swept around the room. 'Oh, God, yes, there he is, in all his princely splendour. That tan is sinful! Why don't I ever get a tan? I can sit in the sun for days and all I do is burn.'

'Shut up, Anne.'

Anne laughed. 'What's he doing here?'

'I don't know. I don't like it.' Daniella felt a knot of apprehension in the pit of her stomach. His appearance in the gallery felt like an intrusion; this was her domain; she didn't want him here, poisoning the atmosphere.

'Maybe he's checking up on you,' Anne suggested. 'Seeing if anything illicit is going on behind the counter here, or in the back room. Maybe he's worried you're cheating on his father with some handsome young stud.'

'You've got a depraved mind.'

Anne grinned. 'It's called artistic imagination.'

Marc approached them. Daniella took a deep breath, trying to keep calm.

'May I help you, sir?' Anne asked, all professional courtesy.

'No, thank you. I'd just like a word with Daniella.' He turned to her, unsmiling. 'I'll buy you lunch; we have something to discuss.'

'I can't leave.'

Anne smiled politely. 'I'm afraid she's needed here.' Anne was a real trooper, not averse to a blatant lie in times of dire emergency!

He regarded her coolly. 'Forgive me if I'm wrong, but you don't appear to be overworking yourselves here.'

Anne's smile vanished and her brown eyes were hotly furious. 'I don't believe that's any of your business, sir. As I said, Daniella stays here.'

He was behind the counter before Daniella realised it. His arm clamped around her shoulders like a vice, immobilising her. 'You can come with me quietly, or you can create a scene—whichever one you prefer.' His tone was low and deadly. 'I suggest the first.'

CHAPTER SIX

DANIELLA stared at Marc in stunned disbelief. His face was very close, his body touching hers as he held her. She could feel his warmth, smell the scent of his aftershave.

'What?' She couldn't believe what she was hearing.

'You heard me. Now come with me quietly—your friend Andrew might not like a scandal in his beloved gallery.'

How right he was. She glanced around. Seven people in search of a quiet lunch hour: his timing was perfect. She felt helpless—helpless and small next to Marc's big, strong body. She gritted her teeth and glared at him.

Anne glared too, with fierce dark eyes. 'I'll call the police,' she said through clenched teeth.

His mouth turned down. 'The Washington police have better things to do. Don't dramatise—I'll have her back within the hour, without a scratch on her shiny exterior.'

At a loss, Anne gave Daniella a searching look. Daniella shrugged. 'He likes these caveman tactics. Don't worry—hold the fort. I'll be back.'

Marc released his grip on her. She took her handbag, swung it over her shoulder, and headed for the door. Marc followed her.

Outside, she squinted against the bright spring light as Marc took her arm. 'This way.'

She shook off his arm and followed him to the car park at the end of the street and to his blue Volvo. She settled herself into the passenger's seat without a word; she was not going to give him the satisfaction of asking where he was taking her for lunch. A hot dog stand on Constitution Avenue, for all she cared.

As it turned out, he did not take her to any restaurant at all, but parked in the underground garage of a luxury block of flats.

Still silent, she preceded him into the entrance hall which was all glass and shiny chrome and potted palms. Marc nodded at the doorman, who greeted him with a smile. It was all very chic. They got into the lift and she watched him punch in the eleventh floor. She was beginning to be curious—were they having lunch at someone's house? She frowned. She couldn't imagine it.

The lift stopped. The doors slid open noiselessly and they stepped out into another, smaller entrance hall. Plush carpeting, more potted plants. Doors. Marc produced a set of keys. She followed him through one of the doors.

No one was in the flat, that much was clear right away. The furnishings were luxurious, but the place had an unlived-in look about it and the air was stuffy.

'What do you think?' he asked.

'Of what?'

'This place. Look around; don't be shy.'

She laughed. 'You've got to be kidding. Why should I want to look around somebody else's apartment?'

'It isn't anybody else's house, at least not in that sense. No one lives here.'

'That's what I thought.'

'You can have it,' he said coolly. 'Plus three thousand dollars a month spending money.'

She was getting better at controlling herself, but for a moment she was incapable of speech.

'You'll stay away from my father, of course,' he went on. 'You'll have your freedom. No need to cater to an old man.'

Keep calm, her inner self warned. Without answering she moved around the room, gearing up for another performance. It was getting easier all the time. She'd given a lot of performances when she was younger—it had been necessary then, too, as a cover-up to hide her feelings. Don't show them you're hurting. Don't show them you're angry. Don't show them you're scared.

She frowned, feigning serious thought. 'What about the utilities—water, electricity?'

His jaw hardened. 'It's all included.'

She nodded, fingering the leaves of a large ficus plant. 'It's silk—I like real plants, not fake.'

'Buy them.' His tone was hard and cold.

She sat down in a chair, crossed her legs and looked around expansively. 'Not bad, but I don't like those curtains.'

'Change them. Send me the bill.' He was getting angry, very angry. It was odd, this sense of power she felt. She couldn't help herself.

'Is there a whirlpool bath?' she asked.

'Yes.'

She jumped up. 'Let me have a look at the rest of the place.'

It was as luxurious as the living-room, and obviously professionally decorated.

'I could learn to like this,' she said agreeably, 'with some changes of course.'

He glared at her, not answering. He was trying to keep his anger in check and he wasn't having an easy job of it.

She sat down again in the living-room. 'That sun-lounge will work as a studio, I think—there's lots of light.'

'That's why I picked this place.'

'How considerate,' she said sweetly. She swung her leg lazily back and forth. 'Will you give me a contract?'

'Yes,' he bit out.

'Good. That's always better with this kind of arrangement, for both parties.'

She jumped up again, restlessly, stood in front of the large window and examined the view. Below, the Potomac River shimmered in the warm spring sunlight, the wooded banks green with new leaves. After a moment, she turned to face him. 'So, if I understand this correctly, instead of being Hayden's kept woman, I'll be yours? Is that it? Interesting, come to think of it. What do you want from me in return apart from the usual? Do we entertain? Do I accompany you to the theatre?'

'No,' he said between clenched teeth. 'Not the usual, not the entertaining, not anything. I'll be in Africa, which isn't far enough away from you.'

She threaded her fingers through her hair, fluffing the curls. 'The only requirement then is that I stay away from your father?'

'Exactly.'

She gave him a worried frown. 'What if he doesn't stay away from me?'

'You will make it clear to him that you no longer want his company. I'm sure you can find a way to convince him.'

'I see. Did you discuss this with your father?'

'No.'

She nodded. 'I didn't think so.' She glanced around again, pretending to consider. 'I'll need some time to think about it.'

'No.' Steely eyes looked at her grimly. 'We did that once. You decide now.'

'You're being unreasonable,' she said calmly, wondering what it was in herself that wanted to goad him, to make him angry. It wasn't an attractive trait, was it? She was getting to know a different side of herself and she wasn't altogether pleased. It was some sort of perverse defence mechanism, a way to cover up her real feelings. Maybe she wanted to hurt him because he was hurting her. Hurting her beyond redemption. How could he? How could he believe she was what he thought she was?

'I want an answer now,' he said. He stood legs apart, hands in his pockets, solid and immovable. 'A better offer you'll never get.'

She shrugged. 'It all depends on what you call "better", isn't it? On what you value in life.'

His eyes narrowed. 'We know what you value in life.'

For a silent moment she studied his hard, angry face. 'Maybe you're wrong,' she said quietly.

His mouth turned down. 'Will you accept?'

He didn't care; his mind was made up. She pushed down the despair, grasping again for composure—the shield of her act to hide behind.

She sighed elaborately. 'It's an interesting offer, really, and you must have put in quite some effort, but I can't accept. You're very generous, but no, thanks. I think I'd rather stay at the house.'

The silence was electric. For a moment she thought Marc would explode, but to her surprise she saw something other than the expected rage in his expression. He seemed stunned and then, for a fleeting moment, she thought she saw a glimmer of doubt, but perhaps she was wrong. His face straightened, his eyes were clear and without expression.

'What is it that you want?' he said at last, his voice low.

She smiled. 'Your father.'

When she got back to the gallery, she was shaking so hard she could barely speak. She wasn't sure how she had managed to make it back, but somehow she'd walked out of the flat, gone down in the lift, and hailed a taxi.

Anne gave her a glass of water. 'What the hell did he do to you?'

'Well, he didn't feed me lunch.' Daniella gulped some water. 'Listen to this. You're not going to believe this.' She told the story with Anne staring at her wide-eyed and stupefied.

'Good God, he really wants you out of the way.'

'In the worst way.'

Anne began to laugh. 'You asked for a contract? Where did you get that idea?'

Despite herself, Daniella laughed too. 'From a movie. It was about these women who are professional mistresses, not out of love or anything, but because a man often wants somebody convenient and discreet on the side who's not going to disrupt his marital life. The men set them up in apartments and give them an allowance, or salary—whatever you call it—and it's all taken care of in a contract, like a business arrangement.' She choked back a laugh. 'I thought it was a nice touch, asking for it.'

'A brilliant idea.' Anne's tone was dry. 'Now he'll never believe you're not a professional.'

'Oh, be quiet, Anne.'

'I'm right, aren't I?'

'It's so stupid. *Why* is he so stupid?'

'Maybe some exotic African virus attacked his brain.'

Daniella sighed. 'I couldn't blame him for that, could I?'

Anne gave her a half-smile. 'No. You'd have to forgive him.'

Daniella grimaced. 'I don't want to forgive him. I'm not that tolerant and gracious.'

'You've got too much pride, that's your problem.'

Too much pride. That night as she lay in bed, Daniella thought about Anne's comment. Pride was the only thing that had saved her. If she hadn't had it, she would still be living with her old grandfather who would regularly take his belt to her and somehow she would think she deserved it. Because, after all, who was she? Just a bastard child whose father had walked off and never taken responsibility for her. If Daniella hadn't been born, her mother might have made something of herself—that was what her grandfather had accused her of over and over again. Her mother had been in her second year in college, the family's pride, when she'd got pregnant by a fellow student. She'd dropped out, come back home and from then on everything had gone downhill.

'I didn't ask to be born,' Daniella would say to her grandfather, feeling the injustice of the accusation down to the depths of her little soul even at an early age. He didn't like her answering back and out would come his hand, or his belt, or whatever was handy. She'd learned to shut up, but inside she'd never capitulated to his verbal and physical abuse. She'd learned to protect herself; she was a survivor.

She would survive this too. After all, who was Marcus Penbrooke anyway? She stared at the bedroom ceiling. Tears welled up in her eyes and she hugged herself hard. 'Oh, damn you, Marc,' she whispered.

* * *

'I need to get away for a little while,' she told Andrew
two weeks later. The strain of living in the same house
with Marc was getting to her. Hayden's observant eyes
had noticed something amiss. He was worrying about
her and soon he was going to want to know what was
wrong. She looked at Andrew pleadingly. 'Can you do
without me for a week or so?'

He frowned. 'Now?'

'No, no. I'll wait till after the opening of the Stromsky
show. I'll paint and hang and all the rest. Anne says it's
OK with her.'

'All right then. Where are you going? St Barlow?'

'I like it there.'

'So do I,' he said drily. 'Can I come too?'

Last summer, at Hayden's invitation, Andrew, Anne
and several of her other friends had all had their vacation
at the villa on the island. It had been wonderful to be
able to share the place with her friends, but this time
she wanted to be by herself.

'I need to be alone,' she said. If Andrew came along,
things might become complicated.

He gave a long-suffering sigh. 'No time anyway. Go
ahead, have a ball, just don't let C.B. Cats talk you into
taking his paintings back with you.'

She laughed. 'You should give him a show. Title it
Life On The Islands. Lots of people would come and
see his stuff.'

He groaned. 'I'd be ruined, sweetheart.'

'You've got no guts,' Anne said, egging him on. 'Take
a risk, live a little.'

'Have you seen his paintings?'

'I was there, remember?'

'You're depraved,' he said, and walked off.

Anne sighed. 'I wish I could come with you. I had a great time last year—meeting C.B. Cats was an adventure.'

Daniella laughed. C.B. Cats was a good-for-nothing tramp who imagined himself a painter. He'd come to the island some ten or twelve years earlier after he'd been involved in some shady land development dealings in his home town in Texas. He painted lurid pictures of nude scenes and beach orgies and whatever else he thought foreign visitors might enjoy. He carted them all over the islands, selling them to the tourists. When he'd received word that a Washington DC gallery owner was among the visitors in the Penbrooke villa, he'd lugged his stuff up the hill and tried valiantly to persuade Andrew to display his paintings.

'Sure,' Andrew had said, smiling charmingly. 'When hell freezes over, Mr Cats.'

Ten days later, after a very successful opening of the Stromsky show, Daniella was in her room, packing for her trip to St Barlow. She wouldn't need much—just some shorts and tops, a bikini and one good dress in case Eve or one of her other friends on the island decided to give a party. She smiled, thinking of Eve with her handicapped leg who spent hours each day giving physical therapy to handicapped children in the island orphanage. Here was someone you could really admire. Spoiled little rich Eve could easily be living it up in Rio or Paris instead.

Daniella put some shorts and shirts in the suitcase on the bed, then riffled through her clothes in the wardrobe looking for a dress.

So many beautiful dresses, shoes, handbags. A nice car in the garage. So much money. Money from a father

her mother had never mentioned, a father she had secretly fantasised about all her young years.

Then one day, two years ago, she'd found out everything. One evening, Julie had called her to tell her that her grandfather had died. It had taken all Daniella's strength to go back to her home town to take care of things. After the funeral, as she'd cleared out the ramshackle house, she'd found the small box—a cheap metal cash box that had belonged to her mother.

Letters. A photograph of a young man, smiling, lounging against a sleek, shiny car. Blond hair falling over a high forehead, piercing blue eyes.

From the letters, Daniella pieced the story together— it wasn't hard. The same centuries-old tale of money and power and prestige. Two lovers: one rich, one poor. Her father, twenty-two years old at the time, could not marry her pregnant mother, who was a little nobody from a poor town. He'd tried to send her money instead. Daniella's mother had kept the letters but not the money. Not a cent of it.

Daniella had come back to Washington, shaken. She had a name. She had a picture. Somewhere, she had a father. With Hayden's contacts, the search had not been long or difficult, but all her hopes had been dashed with the news that her father had died four months earlier. His lawyers, however, had been delighted to hear from her.

Daniella closed her eyes and sighed. She'd wanted a father, but instead she'd found a fortune. Not a large one, perhaps, by some standards, but to her it was unimaginable to have so much money. Yet even now, all the pain of her childhood was no fair trade and she would have gladly given up every cent to have had a real father who'd loved her and her mother, to have had a real home, as Julie had. But her father had thought of her in his will, which was at least an indication that, no matter what, he had never forgotten her, even though he had never even met her. The lawyers had told her he had left a wife, but no other children. She had no half-brothers or half-sisters. No family.

Having finished packing, Daniella closed the suitcase and set it near the door. She'd packed a block of paper and some water colours, charcoal and ink. There were other supplies at the villa. She'd have to spend much of her time painting, hoping the peace and quiet of the island would inspire her to do some good work for the approaching show. After she came back home there wouldn't be much time left. Every time she thought of the show, she could feel herself tense with nerves.

She heard the taxi honk outside and she picked up the suitcase and rushed down the stairs and out of the front door. She'd already said goodbye to Hayden when he'd left for work that morning, and earlier to Mrs Bell and Cora Lee.

Marc was outside, playing ball with Gregory, and he glanced over at her with a frown. She hadn't mentioned her trip to him, so it was possible he didn't even know she was leaving.

'Where are you going?' he demanded, eyes on her suitcase.

'Away,' she said coolly, handing her suitcase to the taxi driver.

Marc turned to Gregory. 'Go to the kitchen and ask Mrs Bell for a couple of Cokes, will you?' The boy nodded and disappeared from view. Marc's gaze returned to Daniella. 'You're leaving?' There was an odd expression in the grey eyes, a mixture of surprise, disbelief, and something else she couldn't identify.

'Yes,' she said. 'Aren't you happy? I'll be out of your way.' She didn't mention for how long. Let him think it was for good.

The driver had deposited the suitcase in the boot and was holding the car door open for her. She made a move to seat herself, when Marc's hand shot out and took her arm, detaining her.

'Where are you going?'

'Far away from you,' she said sweetly, 'just as you wanted. Now let go of my arm.'

He didn't. 'Where?' he bit out.

'It's none of your business,' she said, forcing the words out between clenched teeth. Her arm was hurting. He was making her mad. The poor taxi-driver was looking uncomfortable.

Marc moved and before she could do anything about it, he'd taken hold of her handbag and opened it. The tickets were there, right inside and it didn't take him more than a moment to find out exactly where she was going. He put them back into the bag and handed it over. 'Have a good time,' he said, pseudo-friendly. 'Get yourself a good tan.'

Arriving at Miami airport, several hours later, she was still seething. The *gall* of the man!

The flight from Washington had been on time and she had two hours to kill before boarding the plane to St Barlow. She had a cup of barely drinkable coffee, wandered aimlessly through the duty-free shops and finally settled in a chair at the departure gate to do some people-watching.

People in suits, people in shorts. An Indian lady in a sari. An Arab in flowing robes. Across from her sat an elderly couple, holding hands. Daniella observed them unobtrusively. They seemed excited and worried at the same time. Perhaps this was their first trip to the Caribbean, probably to Jamaica, where the plane would make a stop. Not many tourists came to St Barlow. She watched the old hands, clasped together. They were talking quietly and she could not hear what they were saying. The man was smiling reassuringly at his wife. They looked as if they'd been married for decades and were comfortable with each other, still loving each other.

Daniella felt a painful longing. How wonderful to be married for such a long time and still love each other, to be together all your life. Would she ever have that kind of happiness? Her mother had been alone, terribly alone, and at times Daniella knew a wrenching fear that she, too, would never find the happiness of having a husband and a family. It was what she wanted more than anything: someone to love forever, children, a home with love and joy. Just plain old-fashioned happiness. Was it too much to ask?

Marc was the first man she'd ever fallen in love with. The boys in high school had seemed immature and worried about things that seemed irrelevant to her. Also, she'd been so busy, working every day after school in the local chemist to keep herself in clothes and to have money for art supplies. The rest of the time she would do her schoolwork and paint. After she'd left her grandfather's house, it had been much the same story. She wasn't interested in the men she met at the hotel cocktail lounge where she worked. Besides, she was working day and night saving her money.

Marc was different. With Marc she could talk about her painting, about her dreams for the future. Marc had fascinated her and his kindness and consideration were like a balm on her scruffy little soul. But that was three years ago. No longer did Marc seem the generous, warm-

hearted man she had known him to be—the man she
had fallen in love with.

When she thought of the future, there was always this
picture of herself and Marc and the children they would
have. She could never imagine herself with someone else,
not even after three years.

It's because you were a besotted young thing, she said
to herself. Because he was the first man you loved. Because you're stupid to hang on to crazy, romantic dreams
that can never come true.

She was young, there would be other men. There
would be someone who loved her true self, who would
not be blinded by prejudices and newspaper articles.

The old man sitting across from her put his arm
around his wife's shoulder and kissed her on her wrinkled
cheek. Daniella saw them through a haze of tears. She
got to her feet and walked away, finding a seat across
from a teenage punk with green and purple hair, a dog
collar around his neck and a skull earring in his left ear.
He was a lot easier to look at.

She arrived at the villa late in the afternoon, wel-
comed by a smiling Mrs H. Nobody seemed to know
what her surname was, only that it was very long and
quite unpronounceable. Mrs H. was the housekeeper who
kept the villa in tip top shape all year around, aided by
Mr H., her husband, who was the gardener and general
handyman.

Mrs H. commented that Daniella looked too pale and
too thin. To Mrs H., anyone not black and weighing less
than two hundred pounds was too pale and too thin.
Obviously, Daniella had been working too hard and not
eating enough. Or was it something else? She looked at
Daniella shrewdly and placed her hand on her ample
bosom. 'I'm thinking maybe your heart is paining you?'
she suggested.

Daniella couldn't help but laugh. 'Only a little,' she conceded. 'Some sun, a little rum punch and your cooking and I'll have it fixed in no time.'

If only she could believe it herself.

Daniella carefully picked her way down the rocky path that curved and twisted down the hill to the beach. Fiery red blossoms of a large spreading flamboyant tree contrasted brightly against the cobalt sky and for a moment she stood still, taking in the view, and absorbing the colours of sea and sky and hills and flowers—a myriad of greens and blues, a range of pinks and purples and whites.

She'd slept long and deeply the previous night, the sound of the waves washing ashore a soothing background music. She'd spent the day painting while Mrs H. had tried to fatten her up in the space of one day, bringing her snacks and drinks every hour on the hour: coconut biscuits, pineapple cake, rum pudding, fruits and juices. Daniella smiled to herself. Being small and slim had its advantages; it brought the best out in maternal, nurturing women like Mrs H. and Mrs Bell. She liked being spoiled and it made them happy when she let them.

The breeze from the sea touched her warm cheek and she smelled the salty tang of the water. Taking a deep breath, she felt the tension flow out of her. This place was paradise.

Her gaze swept up to the white house on the hill and she smiled. The whole house to herself. She would be able to calm herself down, feel like herself again, clear her mind of Marc. She would paint the most inspired pictures. All day, she'd felt her spirits rising. Slowly, she continued down the rough path until she reached the small cove. She took off her sandals and walked through the sand, taking pleasure in the soft, powdery feel of it under her feet. It was such a difference from the feel of cool, dewy grass on a summer's morning at home, yet equally sensuous. She spread out the straw mat she'd taken from the house and sat down, hugging her knees, savouring the sight of the placid turquoise sea that lay like a sparkling jewel at her feet.

On both sides of the cove, walls of rock rose up high, greenery growing valiantly from cracks and crevices. It was a very private, secluded place and the only access was by path from the house or by boat from the sea.

She splashed out into the water, swam and floated on the waves. She was not a strong swimmer, but she enjoyed the water. After a while she waded out again and lay down on the mat to dry. The sun was losing its strength and the breeze was on her wet skin. Shadows were creeping up over the sand.

She didn't know what made her look up towards the house, some instinct, a premonition.

A man was coming down the path wearing dark swimming trunks and a red towel slung over his shoulder. Her heart turned over; the breath caught in her throat and for a moment she forgot to breathe. It couldn't be... Oh, please, no, it couldn't be!

She watched him as he came closer, the muscles in his brown legs bunching and relaxing with each step down the rocky trail. His arms swung easily by his side, his body all confident, fluid movement. He had reached the sand and was coming towards her now, the golden glow of the setting sun bronzing his brown skin. The ocean, rock and sky formed a natural backdrop for his virile, muscled torso. From hidden depths she felt a warm tide of primitive desire rush through her body. For one wild and crazy moment, all sanity seemed to have deserted her and her heart pounded in her chest like a frantic bird.

Then other emotions took over: shame and disgust, fury mixed with the pain of lost hope. How dared he? How dared he follow her here when she wanted to be alone? How dared he do this to her?

'Well, hello there,' he said casually. 'How's the water?'

'Why can't you leave me in peace?' she demanded, hearing the anger in her voice—anger touched with despair. 'I came here to get away from you, don't you know that?'

'Is that right?' He regarded her coolly. 'Or is it because you're expecting company that you don't want me around?'

'Company?'

He frowned, quasi-serious. 'Let's see. Perhaps a romantic get together with oh...let's see...Andrew, perhaps?'

Rage nearly choked her. She hated him, she hated this whole sorry situation. 'I came here to be alone! But even if I was expecting someone else, what business is it of yours?'

'Oh, it's my business all right.'

'And you're here to take care of it?'

'Actually, I'm here to deal with the leak in the roof. Apparently there were some problems and, since I have some time, I suggested that I oversee the work and get it done before the rainy season.'

She gritted her teeth. 'I could have done that.'

He shrugged. 'My father forgot about it.'

'He could have called me.'

He smiled, but it didn't reach his eyes. 'Maybe he feels more comfortable with me doing it.'

'Baloney. I'm perfectly capable and he knows it. I've come here several times a year for three years and I have some idea of how the place works, and how to get things done.' She took a deep breath. 'I'm not stupid.'

'Oh, no. I never accused you of that, did I?'

'I hate you,' she said in a choked voice, the words out before she could control herself. 'You're so goddamned arrogant and sanctimonious and you have no idea how stupid you are, how ignorant and ridiculous! You don't know anything! You...oh, to hell with you!' She turned, her eyes blurred by tears and raced away into the water.

CHAPTER SEVEN

HE raced after her, grabbing her in an iron grip. 'I'm stupid, am I? I'm ignorant? So educate me!'

'Let go of me!' She stood up to her thighs in the water, her feet unsteady on the shifting sand beneath and she had no leverage to pull herself free. His grip held her easily and his eyes bored into hers.

'What is it that I don't know?' His voice was calmer now.

'You don't know *me*! You don't know anything about me!' She heard the loss of control in her own voice, but she seemed unable to do anything about it.

'Oh, but I do,' he drawled, letting go of her. 'You're the poor little waif without money and a home. Don't make me cry!'

Her blood turned to ice. She'd never asked for pity or sympathy—not from anyone. Her younger years had not been marked by great happiness, but she was doing fine now. She fixed him with a contemptuous stare. 'Did I ever ask you to?'

He smiled now, a crooked little smile. 'No, you're right, you never did. You're pretty tough, aren't you?'

'Oh, I'm tough all right. Tougher than you'll ever know.' She hugged herself, rubbing her upper arms where his grip had left its mark. 'You may think you know me, but you don't.'

For a moment there was silence. 'I thought I did,' he said, at last, and his voice was softer now, almost regretful. The light grey eyes had lost their intensity, seemed oddly dull—but maybe it was just the reflection of the water.

The sound of the sea surrounded them, waves rolling in, breaking. A primeval sound, old as the world. They gazed at each other, remembering, and time seemed to stand still.

'What did you think?' she whispered.

The muscles in his face worked. A drop of water ran down his cheek and he rubbed it away. 'I thought you were special. Bright, warm, enthusiastic. I thought you were a real person.'

Her heart contracted. 'I am a real person,' she said. 'No matter what you think of me, I'm a real person.'

Something stirred in the depths of his eyes. His arms reached out to her, drawing her against him. His skin was wet and slippery, yet she felt the vibrant warmth of it against her own damp skin. Her heart began to beat erratically. Oh, God, I don't want this to happen, she thought. Please don't let me feel this way. It can't be right.

How could she want him, this man who thought the worst of her? This man who thought she was a fortune-hunter, who insulted her. Could memories have so much power? More power than her common sense? Yet rational thought got pushed out of the way by the images of long ago, so firmly implanted in her mind and heart. Images of his smiling face, his laughing eyes. Memories of his kisses and the delirious play of love.

Other times, other places. She closed her eyes, feeling his lips on hers, firm and cool, his body warm and alive against her. The waves washed around them and she could no longer feel her feet. She was floating and there was no time and no space, only awareness of him, and his hands and mouth. The sounds of the sea hypnotised her and there was a deep, swirling desire taking over her being.

She kissed him back, answering the urgent passion in his hands and mouth.

Then a shriek rent the air—an ugly raucous shriek—freezing her blood. She tore herself away and looked up in fear. Overhead in the blue sky a large bird, black as the night, flapped its wings in warning and shrieked again. Then, in a flash, it was gone. Daniella stared into the empty sky, shivering, dazed and disorientated, suddenly not sure she had actually seen the bird. She swayed, off balance in the moving water, aware of no longer being held. Her gaze found Marc, standing in front of her, arms by his side, and a wave of misery and pain flooded her. Tears burned her eyes.

She turned away from him and waded back to the beach, tears streaming down her cheeks. He followed her out. She dried herself off, refusing to meet his eyes, trying desperately to stop the flow of tears. Yet even the water dripping from her hair, down her face, did not hide the fact that she was crying.

'Why are you crying?'

'How *dare* you do this to me?' she said fiercely, almost choking on the words. The shriek of the black bird echoed in her head. 'How dare you kiss me and hold me? You despise me and still you want this from me! What does that make *you*? Think of that!'

He said nothing, his face expressionless—as if he'd pulled it straight by sheer force of will.

She hugged the towel to her chest, as if protecting herself. 'You want to sleep with me—you want my body—don't you dare deny it! What kind of morals do you have? How dare you criticise *me* for *my* supposed sins! If you're so convinced I'm your father's mistress, you might at least show some moral decency yourself and stay away from me!'

She saw him wince and a spasm flashed across his face. Bull's eye! she thought, but it gave her no satisfaction. He wanted her, she knew full well. The terrible thing was that part of her wanted him too. Some blind, romantic part of her still believed in the man of her memories, the man who kept haunting her in her dreams.

Marc took the red towel and rubbed his chest dry, his expression now carefully bland. 'I got the idea you rather enjoyed it yourself,' he said calmly.

She was trembling. 'You wish!' she said with as much force as she could muster. She draped her towel around her neck and slogged off through the sand, up the rocky path leading to the house.

She was furious with him and with herself. She should not have let it happen. Yet she trembled again remembering him holding her in the water, the feel of his mouth, his skin against hers. She closed her eyes and stubbed her toe on a rock, cursing under her breath. He had ruined everything! She had wanted to get away from him and he had followed her. No peace, after all.

Why had he come here? Surely not for the roof? It was just an excuse and she knew it. The spicy smells of Mrs H.'s cooking greeted her, as she entered the house through the back door. She sighed as she moved through the cool hallway to her room at the far end of the house. She'd have to have her dinner with Marc, there was no escaping it.

Her room was spacious and cool. Everything was a pristine white, from the walls to the curtains and bedspread. Even the two rattan chairs and table were painted white. The only colour came from a vivid splash of violet bougainvillaea drooping from a tall glass vase and a large acrylic painting of a Caribbean scene on the wall: people,

buses, trucks, baskets of fruit and painted buildings
spilled their colour into the room. She loved the painting,
feeling the life in it, almost hearing the noise and laughter
it portrayed.

The room had its own bathroom and she stripped off
her bikini and stepped into the shower. She had about
an hour to compose herself before dinner was served
and she was determined not to let Marc get to her again.
For a long time she let the cool water stream over her—
it was soothing and relaxing. She wished she hadn't cried;
she didn't want him to think she still cared or was
vulnerable. It didn't go well with her act, did it? She
was tired of her act—it took too much out of her. She
was tired of all the crazy misunderstandings, of Marc's
blindness. What was the matter with him, anyway? Why
didn't he see? Why didn't he believe her? Couldn't he
see through her act? Marc was a smart man. What made
him so obsessed with her relationship with his father?

Mrs H. had outdone herself with her spicy curried
chicken, but it was hard to enjoy the food sitting across
from Marc. His eyes made her nervous, the memory of
that kiss on the beach glinting in their depths. The
atmosphere was laden with tension and they ate their
meal saying only the most inane things to each other.
Afterwards Daniella took her coffee out to the veranda,
hoping he'd have the good sense to stay away.

The veranda was her favourite place in the house. It
had a view of the sea and the green hills and caught the
ocean breeze. There were rattan tables and chairs and a
lamp so it was possible to read after dark, which fell
early in the tropics.

She had been alone, reading for about an hour, relieved Marc had not made an appearance, when he finally
did show up. He carried a pitcher and glasses. She felt

herself tense as she watched him putting the tray on the table and settling his big frame in a chair.

'I wonder if we could manage a ceasefire,' he said calmly.

She frowned, surprised. 'Why?'

He waved his hand around, his gesture encompassing the island, the sea, the palm trees. 'Is this a place for war?'

Daniella shrugged. 'There have been plenty. What's one more?'

The island had been owned by a succession of colonists, pioneers and pirates—the Spaniards, the Danes, the Dutch and the English. Bloody battles had been fought over the seemingly insignificant heap of rocks, and in the end the English had prevailed. Slaves from West Africa had been imported by the planters in massive numbers to work the sugarcane fields and their descendants now made up the majority of the island's population.

'I wasn't thinking of history,' Marc said. 'I'm thinking of the present. This is a peaceful place. It's been a long time since I was here last.' He frowned. 'The summer before I left for Peru. I always liked being here. Do you come here often?'

'A couple of times a year.'

'Well, let's make the best of it. I'll try and arrange to have the leak in the roof fixed as soon as possible and then I'll leave.'

She scrutinised his face as he waited for a reply—he was lying about the leak. If he wanted to go, he could leave now and she could easily handle the repair, or Mr H. could, for that matter. There was another reason Marc was here. Maybe he was just waiting to see if Andrew would show up, or some other man. Whatever the reason, she didn't trust his motives.

She shrugged indifferently. 'Sure,' she said lightly.

He lifted the pitcher. 'You want some of Mrs H.'s rum punch?'

'Please.'

He poured the drinks and handed her a glass, then took his own and lifted it. 'Let's drink to peace.'

She wished she knew why he was suddenly so interested in peace. Had he forgotten *he* was the one who had declared war? And there couldn't be peace, not until he realised how wrong he had been from the beginning.

Marc was not present at breakfast, nor at lunch, much to her relief. She spent the morning painting, and in the afternoon she went to the orphanage in town, driving one of the two little Mini Mokes parked in the garage. It was a crazy little vehicle with a canvas top and no sides. It looked more like a toy car built from a kit than a serious mode of transport and Daniella enjoyed driving it. It went well with the sunny, happy ambience of the island.

She spent several hours with Eve, helping her with the children, playing with them. Afterwards they went back to the resort hotel, the only one on the island, owned by Eve's father. Eve ordered them a proper English afternoon tea with scones and cream and the whole works, an island tradition left over from colonial times and one that Daniella enjoyed thoroughly.

Daniella found Marc home for dinner that evening and somehow they managed to have a half civilised conversation over the breaded, flying fish Mrs H. served them. Apparently, he seemed determined not to insult or antagonise her. Thank God for small mercies, she thought wryly.

He accompanied her to the veranda for coffee, bringing the local newspaper with him, which he shared with her. They talked about the island and the people they knew, until the quiet of the evening was disturbed by the asthmatic sputtering of a car labouring up the hill towards the house.

Marc glanced over at her, one eyebrow cocked. 'Who could that be?'

She had friends on the island and they knew she was here; it could be anyone. She was aware of Marc's suspicions and a terrible thought occurred to her. Her stomach churned with anxiety. What if Andrew had got it into his head to hop on a plane and come to see her? Maybe he thought the romantic atmosphere of the island was more conducive to his mission of getting her into bed?

She had not invited him but, if it was Andrew coming up the hill in a decrepit local taxi, Marc would never believe she hadn't asked him to come. Well, so be it, she thought philosophically. There are other things he doesn't believe, either. One more won't make any difference.

The car stopped and moments later there were voices and the slamming of a car-door. The wooden stairs leading up to the veranda from outside began to creak under the weight of several pairs of feet. A puffy red face on a thick neck and heavy shoulders came into view. Sweating, cursing and gasping for air, the man hauled the rest of his body up on to the veranda. He wore enormous, flowered shorts and an unbuttoned blue shirt that revealed a soft, hairless chest and a quivering belly. Andrew he was not. Daniella bit her lip, suppressing a laugh.

Behind the man trotted a girl of about twenty with frizzy red hair. She wore shapeless white shorts and a yellow tank top and she held a large flashlight in her hand. The unlikely pair was accompanied by a young black boy carrying a flat bundle wrapped in plastic. The girl and the boy remained standing in the shadows while the big man lumbered forward.

There was no doubt about it, it was C.B. Cats.

Marc stared at him in stony silence. The man mopped his forehead with a handkerchief and sagged down into a chair, uninvited. 'Lordie, Lordie, ah just about got me a heart attack climbin' those stairs!' He looked at Daniella with a grin. 'Why, howdy, ma'am. Ah'm Cats. C.B. Cats. Ah believe we met last year?'

'Yes.'

'Ah'm an ole friend of Marc here. Thought ah'd pay mah respects.'

Marc rose slowly to his feet, his expression showing no delight at seeing his 'ole' friend. 'How did you know we were here?' His voice was hard, lacking all welcome.

The man laughed uproariously. 'Coconut telegraph, haw, haw, haw! We got our ways on this godforsaken rock, haw, haw, haw!'

Marc was not amused. 'What do you want?'

C.B. Cats ignored him and fixed his eyes on Daniella. 'Is the big boss here?'

'Mr. Penbrooke?'

'No. Andrew Benedict. I got something special for him. Something real special.'

'We're not interested,' Marc said coldly. Daniella felt a flare of annoyance. What did he mean, *we*? Cats hadn't come to see Marc, so why didn't he stop interfering? Still, it seemed better not to make a point of it now. To be truthful, she wasn't sure she'd be able to get rid of the man by herself. She watched Marc eyeing the fat man as if he were a slug in a strawberry patch. 'Nobody here is interested in your paintings,' he said with distaste. 'Go peddle them somewhere else.'

Obviously Marc was quite familiar with Cats' private brand of art.

The man laughed hoarsely, undaunted. 'You'll be interested in these, ole buddy.' He turned to the boy. 'Amos, bring 'em over here.'

The young boy scooted forward with his flat bundle, glancing over at Marc with a look of fear in his dark eyes. With swift movements he removed the plastic, uncovering several unframed water colour paintings hiding between two pieces of protective cardboard. Carefully he lay them down on one of the coffee-tables.

'Pepper!' Cats bellowed. 'Gimme the flashlight!'

The girl handed it to him silently and retreated again into the shadows. The man shone the beam of light on to the picture on the top.

Daniella scrutinised the paintings one by one, feeling a stirring of excitement. There were four of them: delicate, soft-coloured portrayals of village life—simple scenes of people working, talking, buying and selling in the market, children at play. The flashlight was not producing the most advantageous light but, even so, she could tell that the paintings were certainly worth looking at.

'These are good,' she said, and Marc moved abruptly, picking up the paintings and carrying them into the house. She followed him in, Cats plodding behind her, wheezing ominously.

Marc turned on the light and, for a few silent moments, they examined the paintings a little closer. There was nothing at all here that resembled the crude, garish paintings Cats had shown her and Andrew last year. She turned to Cats. 'Who did these?' she asked.

Cats laughed a low, rumbling laugh. 'Me.' He jabbed a stubby finger at the lower right hand corner of one of the paintings. 'See? It says raht here: C.B. Cats.'

'I can read,' she said coolly.

'You lying son of a bitch,' Marc said in a low, dangerous tone. 'This is not your work.'

Cats' eyebrows rose in indignation. 'It ain't? Why, you sayin' ah'm a liar?'

'You got it.' Marc eyed him with cold dislike.

Cats shook his head in dismay. 'Why, ah'm real disappointed, ole buddy! We've known each other a long time and...'

'Exactly,' said Marc, the one word carrying a wealth of meaning. He rested his hands on his hips, eyes contemptuous.

Cats' fleshy chest quivered as he heaved a heavy sigh of resignation. 'Ah, well, so what? What difference does it make?'

'I'm sure you wouldn't understand, you fraud. Now take this stuff and get out of here.'

Cats squared his shoulders. 'Ah didn't come here to ask your opinion. If Benedict ain't here, maybe the lady here is interested. She works for him.' He nodded in Daniella's direction.

Marc took a step forward. 'I want you out of here.'

Daniella held up her hand. 'Wait a minute. Whose paintings are these?'

Cats shrugged. 'Friend of mine. And there's more.'

'And he wants to sell them?'

'Yeah.'

'So why is your name on them?'

He gave a sly grin and shrugged.

Daniella gave him a disgusted look. 'You're a crook. Andrew would never do business with you.'

'Ah'll make him a good deal, you tell him that.'

'What about your ethics, your principles, Mr Cats?' she asked. 'Doesn't that bother you just a little bit?'

He laughed. 'Not much, honey. You can't sell principles for money.'

'You're a cynic, Mr Cats.'

He smiled good naturedly. 'Just a realist, honey.'

The man was a lost cause, she should have known that already. 'Well, unfortunately for you, Mr Benedict has his standards. You'll have to make your deals somewhere else, and I feel sorry for your friend. I think his work is good. Too good for a crook like you to peddle it.'

Cats' eyes narrowed. 'Well, if you're not interested, that's fahn bah me. I'll take 'em to Barbados. I know a place there——'

'You do that,' Marc cut in. 'Now get out of here, or I'll throw you out! I don't want to see your face again unless you have the artist with you.'

'Well, that maht be a little difficult.'

'I'm not surprised.' Marc took the paintings and strode through the door back to the verandah. The girl and the boy were still standing in the same place.

Cats wrapped the plastic back around the paintings. He threw Marc a vicious look. 'You think you're such hot stuff, don't you, ole boy? Well, lemme tell you something. Without your rich daddy you'd be nothing. You'd be a loser. You'd be...'

Marc made one swift movement towards Cats and the man took to his heels. The party disappeared hastily down the stairs and Marc sat back down in his chair. The car engine sputtered reluctantly into life and a few moments later the sound of the retreating vehicle faded into the night.

Daniella bit her lip, trying not to laugh. She glanced over at Marc, meeting his eyes. He was grinning. She began to laugh. 'Oh, my, I thought you were mad as hell.'

'The man is a joke.'

'And a fraud and a crook.'

'I'm glad you agree with me. I apologise for interfering; I realise he didn't come to see me, but he rubs
me up the wrong way and frankly I don't want him in
the house.'

'I was just as happy to see him go.' She smiled, seeing
again the strange scene with the rowdy Cats, the silent
girl and the scruffy little boy with the fear in his eyes.
'I wonder if he really thought Andrew or I would think
he'd painted those pictures.'

'He didn't really care, as long as Andrew was going
to buy them and sell them for big money in his fancy
gallery.'

'And he would have paid his friend a pittance and
kept the rest.' She sighed. 'That's really too bad. I wish
we could find out who did them.'

'Do you think Andrew would be interested?'

'Not for his own gallery, no, but there might be a way
to help sell them somewhere else. They're really quite
good, but Andrew would find them too...simple, and
lacking in technique.' She grinned. 'That's what he said
of my work in the beginning.'

'But not any more?'

'He says I've matured a lot and my technique has improved dramatically. In his opinion my themes are more
interesting and innovative and I...I show great promise.'
It embarrassed her a little to say this. She shrugged
lightly. 'What can I say? He's the expert. My show will
tell; we'll see if anyone agrees with him.'

They talked about her painting, the house, the island,
their voices low in the warm night air. She was suddenly
aware how peaceful it was to sit here with him, surrounded by the sounds of insects and the sea breeze
rustling the palm fronds. She smelled the incense of the

mosquito coils, a fragrance she always associated with the warm, languorous nights of the tropical island. They'd never been together here and she felt an odd sensation, as if together they were caught in some magical spell, a separate paradise where no anger existed and where the past was forgotten. She felt a sudden aching longing for the nightmare of the past weeks to be gone, erased from her memory and from his.

'Are you dreaming?' he asked softly, and she looked up in surprise, feeling warmth flooding her face. He laughed softly. 'I was asking you if you'd care for some rum punch.'

'Sorry,' she muttered. 'I didn't hear you. Yes, please, I'd like some.'

He came to his feet and went into the house. She got up and leaned against the veranda railing and looked out over the dark, tranquil sea. Small lights blinked here and there. Boats. Maybe yachts or fishing boats. Hayden's yacht lay moored in the marina. Whenever he was on the island they would take it out to sea and enjoy the quiet of the water, sail to other islands and often invite friends to come along.

Not so very long ago she would not have dreamed this would be part of her life. In her teenage years she'd had many dreams, but none of riches and glamour. She hadn't wanted to be a model or a film star, like some of her friends. She'd dreamed of finding her father, or being a painter, of having a real family.

Not all her dreams had come true, but she had Hayden, and that was certainly some sort of miracle. With Hayden she'd started a life full of caring and support and joy. Painting, studying, plays and concerts and parties. Now she had someone who cared about her, someone she loved for his kindness and interest in her. She lived in a beautiful house, had her own room with her own studio. And this too was part of it, this villa on this exotic island where she loved to come to laze in the sun and paint. She was lucky, so terribly lucky. She leant against the railing and smiled into the dark, hearing the small fruit bats swooping around the banana plants.

Marc came back with two drinks. He handed her a glass and she sat down and drank thirstily. It was icy cold and tartly sweet and tasted deliciously of rum mixed with pineapple, orange and lime and other fruits.

'I'd like to ask you something,' she said, feeling suddenly brave. 'I'd like to know what's going on between you and your father.'

She felt more than saw him tense. He stared off into the night and, in the silence that followed, she wondered if her impulsive question had been a mistake. She drank some more punch, sipping it a little more slowly.

'You don't think I've been much of a son, do you?' Marc asked at last.

Slowly she traced the rim of her glass with her index finger. 'No.'

'Would it surprise you to hear that my father has never been much of a father to me?'

Daniella thought of Hayden's kindness and consideration, the time and effort he had given to help her, all the love he had shown her over the past three years.

'Yes,' she said huskily.

He gave a short, humourless laugh. 'I expected you would say that.'

She met his eyes. 'Why?'

'The man you know is not the same man I knew as a child.'

'He loved you,' she said quietly. 'He loved you and your sister and your mother.'

'We hardly ever saw him,' he said, his voice oddly toneless. 'My father was a very busy man and he was always gone, doing very important things. He had no time to attend my basketball games or my sister's piano recitals. My mother brought us up.' He sighed. 'It's all a long time ago. I learned to make my own way, not to depend on him for support. Of course all his money gave me many advantages and I ended up doing what I wanted to do with my life, which, in the end, is what counts.'

'But not the life your father wanted.'

'No, not the one he wanted.' He tipped his head back and drained his glass. 'You want another one?'

She shook her head. 'No, thanks.'

He disappeared inside. He had no desire to discuss the subject any further, that was clear. It saddened her to think of Hayden being too busy for basketball games and piano recitals. In a sudden flash of insight, she understood why Marc was spending so much time with Gregory: in Gregory he recognised himself as a boy, neglected by a father who was always too busy. She wondered vaguely if Marc, on some unconscious level, envied her for all the attention Hayden was giving her— the help and support he and his sister had never received.

When Marc came back with his drink, she came to her feet. 'I think I'll go to bed; it's getting late.'

'What's the hurry? Stay. Keep me company.'

It was an odd request. 'Why?'

His mouth curved in a half-smile. 'It's a beautiful night. Look at the stars.'

She glanced up at the wide expanse of sky, glittering with points of light. 'I don't know anything about stars,' she said, suddenly regretful. 'Their names, their places. I don't recognise any of them.' She sat down and folded her legs beneath her.

'A serious gap in your education,' he said lightly. 'We should remedy that.'

So, in the sultry tropical night, she listened to him as he talked about stars and constellations, pointing them out and naming them. She was spellbound, feeling a magic weaving itself around them, as she was swept up in the mystery and the beauty of the heavens.

He told her of ancient myths and folk traditions of people around the world—people who had looked at the same sky for thousands of years. They planted and harvested their crops, married and celebrated births according to signs they read in the positions of the stars and constellations.

'How do you know so much?' she asked, amazed at the extent of his knowledge, the fascinating stories he had told her.

He shrugged lightly. 'The nights are long where I live in Africa.'

She imagined him spending hours looking at the sky at night, reading, listening to people telling him stories.

A low rumble intruded into the peaceful sky and moving lights appeared out of nowhere. She followed them with her eyes for a moment and sighed. 'I know the name of that one,' she said, sorry the magic was gone. Suddenly she felt very tired. How long had they been here? She had no idea; she'd forgotten her watch. She unfolded herself from her chair and stood up. 'I'd better go in now.'

Marc came to his feet as well. 'It has got late, hasn't it?' He smiled. 'Goodnight, Daniella.'

She wasn't used to seeing him smile at her like that and, for a moment, she just stood there looking at him, feeling a warm longing well up inside her.

'Thank you.' Her voice sounded husky.

'For what?'

'For showing me the stars.'

There was a dark, intense look in his eyes. His hand reached out and cupped her chin. His touch was electric and every nerve in her body tingled. Slowly his face moved closer and the air around them vibrated with tension. Her heart turned over as she felt his lips on hers in a soft, sensuous kiss.

For one magic moment there was nothing but his kiss, nothing but sheer heady delight, then he drew back. 'Goodnight, Daniella.' His voice was soft, almost husky, and the tone of it hailed back to another time.

Her tongue wouldn't move, so she turned and went inside without a word, the pain of the bitter present overwhelming her.

She dreamed that night of other stars and other skies, of other nights, long ago, when she had loved him. She awoke in the middle of the night, her face wet with tears.

The house was silent and she lay awake for a long time.

Marc lay in bed, pretending desperately he didn't hear her cry. For hours now he'd lain awake, tormented by thoughts and feelings he could make no sense of, thoughts and feelings twisting and turning in his head until he thought he would go crazy. He'd been convinced he'd find Andrew at the villa, but there was no sign of him—nor of any other male for that matter. A discreet telephone call to Washington this morning had established the fact that Andrew was safely ensconced at the Benedict with no plans for a trip anywhere.

Nothing made sense.

Daniella had spent the morning painting and in the afternoon she'd gone to the orphanage, of all places, and spent several hours there helping Eve Ashwell and playing with the children. In the evening she'd been at home and Cats had arrived. Nothing was going on.

Her voice danced in his head, words, phrases coming back to him, haunting him. 'If you're so convinced I'm your father's mistress, you might at least show some moral decency yourself and stay away from me!' 'What about your ethics, your principles, Mr Cats?' 'Doesn't that bother you just a little bit?'

He thrashed around in his bed, unable to sleep. Three years ago he'd fallen hopelessly in love with her, but he'd known he could not possibly ask for commitments then. She was so young, so naïve despite all the sad experiences of her life. She'd told him her story without a trace of self-pity, speaking matter-of-factly, as if she had accepted and come to grips with the life fate had given her. She wanted to be a painter and she'd been full of dreams and hopes. Her courage and enthusiasm had touched him deeply. He thought of the dandelion painting she had given him, heard again the words she had spoken, her face flushed. 'You can't destroy true love, no matter what you do to it.'

That had been three years ago and in that time everything had changed. He'd come back to Washington fully convinced Daniella was the woman the newspapers and the pictures portrayed—in essence if not in detail. Where there was smoke, there was fire. From friends in Washington he heard nothing that contradicted the stories. They'd given him discreet, well-meant warnings. On his return, he had been determined to get Daniella out of his father's life, and out of his own, for good.

He no longer recognised the girl he had left behind. She was mature, sophisticated, confident; she dressed with exquisite taste and seemed perfectly at ease in the circles his father moved in. He thought of her expensive clothes, her car, her jewellery. No way could she afford any of those herself with her part-time job and the few paintings she sold now and then.

The situation was so obvious, so clear. What other explanation could there be? He wanted desperately to believe that he was wrong, that all this was a nightmare of his own creation. He wanted to believe that the spirited girl of three years ago was still there, merely hiding behind that sophisticated façade she had erected as a defence against his accusations.

Yet the doubts remained, and another face flashed briefly through his mind: dark hair, dark eyes. Beautiful Clarissa. He had not grieved for her long: she'd not been worth it. Instead, he'd berated himself bitterly for being so blind, for not having seen through her. Now she was married to another man and all he felt was contempt for the way she lived her life.

He groaned and turned again. He could not afford to be taken in by one more calculating female. Clarissa had fooled him completely. He had vowed it would never happen again.

Still, every time he looked at Daniella, a secret, tenacious corner of his heart kept wanting to see the girl of three years ago, wanting to hold her and kiss her and make love to her. Several times now he'd been overwhelmed by moments of weakness, forgetting everything, his mind blank of all warnings and fears. He'd taken her in his arms, pretending for those few precious moments she was the girl he had loved three years ago.

From the other room he heard her cry. He groaned and buried his face in the pillow.

CHAPTER EIGHT

THE next morning Daniella offered to do the shopping for Mrs H., who said she really only needed fresh fruit.

'I'll go to the market,' Daniella said. 'I want to go into town anyway.'

The capital was the only town on the island, a town like a painting with houses the colour of baby pink, lime, blue or lavender. She wandered through the narrow streets, enjoying the sights, soaking up the atmosphere.

In the crowded open market she bought papaya, mangoes and pineapple, joking with the rotund market women in their colourful flowered dresses and straw hats. The market was one of her favourite places with its noise and laughter and abundance of exotic tropical fruits and vegetables.

It was very hot, and, her purchases made, Daniella found a small outdoor café and ordered a glass of soursop juice. Contentedly sipping the tartly sweet juice, she observed the passers-by.

'Excuse me.' The voice was low and hesitant.

Daniella turned her head, finding the girl, Pepper, standing in front of her, wearing faded red shorts and a black top, with a frayed army-green backpack hanging from her shoulders. 'Hi,' Daniella said. 'Sorry, I didn't see you.'

Pepper ran a hand through her frizzy red hair. 'I wasn't sure it was you at first. It was kinda dark when we came to see you last night.'

'Yes. You want to sit down? Have something to drink?' Pepper had pretty green eyes and a pert little nose.

'Yes, thank you.' Sliding the backpack off, she sat down across from Daniella. 'You know, we were never introduced. Like, I don't even know your name or anything.' She seemed embarrassed. Daniella could understand that. Accompanying Cats on his errand must have been rather humiliating.

'I'm Daniella Michaels. And you're Pepper, right?'

'Yeah.' She wiped her damp forehead with the back of her hand. 'Wow, it's hot!'

Pepper waved at the waiter and ordered a Coke. He was back only moments later with the requested drink, smiling and asking where they were from and how they were liking St Barlow. The island was very small and had not yet attracted many tourists, so foreigners were still a rarity.

'I want to...er...talk to you about the paintings,' Pepper said after he'd gone back to his duties.

'Are they yours?' Daniella couldn't help asking.

Pepper's eyes grew wide and then she laughed. 'Oh, wow! No! I wish, I wish! And if they were, I sure wouldn't have handed them over to that creep Cats! Amos's mother painted them. You know, the little kid that was with us? They live in Cats' village. She had no idea what to do with them and she went to Cats because he's a painter, figuring maybe he could help her sell them. He made her a deal.' She shrugged. 'You know the rest.'

Daniella nodded. 'That's what we figured.'

Pepper sighed. 'I felt bad, you know, but I didn't know what to do about it. Well, I'm leaving this afternoon, so I don't care if Cats finds out that I told you. I don't know if this man—the gallery owner—would want those paintings, but...' She shrugged again. 'I thought they were real good.'

'I liked them too.' They weren't material for Andrew's gallery, but there were other places. 'How do we find her?'

'Just ask for Ernestine. It's a small village, they all know her.' She sucked on her straw and drank half her Coke in one go.

Daniella took a sip of her own drink. The girl intrigued her. 'Why are you telling me this? Isn't Cats your friend?'

Pepper looked indignant. 'My friend? That scumbucket? No way! I stayed with him a couple of days, you know. Like, I kinda ran out of money. He told me he was a painter. Wanted me to model for him. All on the level, you know. I checked it out, sort of. I'm not stupid, you know what I mean? They told me it was true that he was a painter and that he, like, sells his stuff all over the Caribbean. So I figured why not?' She sucked noisily at the straw. 'Ever seen his paintings? They're gross. I mean, really gross!'

Daniella nodded. 'I know, I saw some of them.'

'Pornography, if you ask me. Well, the problem was, like, I had to eat and sleep, you know, so I told him I'd sit for him as long as I could keep my clothes on. Well, at least my bikini. He wasn't too happy, but I guess he figured, like, I'd change my mind or something.' She grinned. 'He doesn't know I'm leaving today. I went to the bank this morning and got the money my old man sent me.'

'Are you going home?'

'Home? To South Dakota? No way! I don't know where I'm going exactly. I'm hitching a ride on a sailing boat with this Indian guy from Trinidad. I love sailing. So peaceful and all. Know what I mean?'

They ordered another drink and Pepper told Daniella the lengthy story of her island-hopping travels: rather bizarre tales which kept Daniella quite amused for more than an hour.

'Well, I gotta go,' Pepper announced finally. She got up and hoisted the pack on to her back. 'It was nice meeting you. Maybe I'll come to Washington some time and look you up.' She swung away down the street with a wave of her hand, leaving Daniella to pay for the drinks.

Daniella drove back to the villa with her purchases and went down to the beach to finish painting a picture she'd started the day before. She felt stimulated and inspired by her walk through town and her visit to the market. The vivacity and colour of the island life never failed to stir up her imagination.

Marc found her later, saying Mrs H. was holding lunch for her, and she looked at him rather befuddled and disorientated. 'Lunch?'

He laughed. 'As in—food and eating. It's almost one. Aren't you hungry?'

She frowned. 'I don't know. I was working.' She stared at the painting, trying to pull herself away.

'It's beautiful,' he said quietly, and she glanced up, suddenly alert.

'It's not finished. I don't like it when people see my work before it's finished.'

'Why not?'

'It's embarrassing.'

He gave her a puzzled frown. 'Why is that embarrassing?'

She shrugged, helpless. 'It's an uncomfortable feeling, because things aren't right yet. The painting may look wrong or dumb, or, oh, I don't know! I just don't like it.'

'OK, OK. Sorry. Let me help you carry this stuff up.'

Lunch was a seafood salad and crusty bread. Daniella watched Marc as he buttered a piece of bread. His hands were big and strong and brown. She took a sip of mineral water and looked away. 'I know who painted those pictures Cats showed us last night,' she said. 'It was a woman in his village.'

He cocked an eyebrow. 'How did you find that out?'

'Oh, I have my ways,' she said, smiling. 'Actually, I ran into Pepper this morning—the girl who was with him—she told me.' Daniella recounted the story.

'Just what we thought,' he said.

'I feel sorry for that woman. Cats will sell those paintings somewhere else and take her to the cleaners. I wish I could help her.'

'Why?' he asked. 'You don't even know her.'

Daniella looked out into the distance. 'She's a village woman, sitting here on this tiny island. The chances are nil that she'll ever get anywhere. I think that's a waste. From what I've seen, she has real talent and I'd like it if I could help her. Give her at least a chance to make some honest money without Cats taking most of it.' She grimaced. 'It makes me mad to think that bum is taking what doesn't belong to him.'

Marc did not respond, and she took a bite of her food and listened to the sounds of the sea and the wind in the palm trees.

'I know what it's like,' she said quietly. 'I got lucky and somebody gave me a break. I have a chance now.'

'Who? Andrew?'

She shook her head. 'No . . . yes. . . . I mean, yes, he's giving me a break now with the group show. But I meant way in the beginning when I came to Washington.' She looked into his eyes. 'Your father helped me.'

His face showed no emotion. 'What did he do?'

'He helped me find the job at the Benedict and he gave me a place to stay.' She didn't care how Marc wanted to interpret that, but it was the truth. 'He had contacts so I had a way in to some places, to display my paintings,' she went on. 'They're in a couple of banks, a real estate office and the showroom of an interior design company. You can't sell your work if you can't display it.' She paused. 'I would like to turn around and do the same for someone else.'

There was another silence. She wondered what he was thinking. She didn't care what he was thinking. She took another bite from her food.

'Would you like us to go and see this woman, this afternoon?' he asked after a while.

She looked at him in surprise. 'You want to come with me?'

He gave a crooked grin. 'Why not? I'm curious, and I've got time on my hands.'

Cats' village lay on the north shore of the island. The curving road meandered through small villages and rich green countryside, now and then offering a spectacular view of the sea, the waters changing from emerald to sapphire to turquoise. They passed through hills, and valleys lush with coconut groves, broken up, here and there, by fields of green waving sugarcane, tall and straight like giant grass. It *was* giant grass, she reminded herself, smiling at nothing in particular.

'This is so beautiful,' she said. 'I never get enough of it, all those different kinds of plants and trees. See that breadfruit tree?'

It was hard to miss; it loomed on the right side of the road, an impressive specimen with large-lobed, glossy green leaves and giant round fruits hanging from the branches. The starchy fruit could weigh up to ten pounds and was used like potatoes—boiled, or fried.

'I made a painting of it once: just a couple of leaves and a part of the fruit and a tiny blue bird for perspective. I did it in acrylics and it was quite exotic.' She remembered the luscious greens, how much work it had been to get them just right, and how wonderful it had been, how wonderful it always was, to see a painting emerge just the way she'd visualised it in her mind.

'Sounds rather Georgia O'Keeffe-ish. Do you still have it?'

She shook her head. 'No. It hung in the interior design store for exactly five days and then they sold it. The man who bought it then took me out to lunch and wanted to see what else I had and bought two more—also island pictures. One was a close-up of the bloom of a banana plant—very strange. Have you ever really looked at one?'

He nodded. 'I've got a mess of them growing by my house in Ghana. I walk past them every day.'

Ernestine was not hard to find. She lived in a small wooden village house, neatly painted a pale pink trimmed with white. Flowered curtains fluttered in and out of the open windows and the laughter of children greeted them as Daniella and Marc opened the gate. A pretty white goat stood tethered to a mango tree and on one side of the house a clump of untidy plantain plants bore a heavy load of fruit.

A tiny girl, hair neatly parted and braided, opened the door and stared at them wide-eyed: white visitors obviously were not a common sight. Moments later a woman in her thirties appeared behind her and greeted them shyly.

Daniella explained their business and she invited them into the small room and offered them tea. It was clean and simply furnished with a small table and a few chairs. A crucifix hung on one wall and a picture of the Virgin Mary on another.

The little girl stood next to Daniella's chair and kept looking at her curiously.

'What's your name?' Daniella asked.

'Maria,' she answered with a half-suppressed giggle. 'Maria, Maria, Maria!' she repeated, skipping out of the room. Daniella could hear her excited chatter in another part of the house.

Ernestine came back into the room with a tea-tray and for the next half-hour they talked about painting and Cats and his shady dealings. Ernestine showed them several more of her paintings, each one better yet than the ones Cats had in his possession. Daniella enjoyed the sing-song tone of Ernestine's island English, and her soft, melodious laugh, and she felt a growing dislike for Cats for trying to take advantage of this woman.

'What I'd like to do,' she explained, 'is take your paintings with me, frame them properly and find a place to display them. I cannot guarantee that they will sell, of course, but I think they will. I know a lot of people who can help me.' She paused. 'What I can do is give you a down-payment now, and then send you the rest later.'

'What about a commission for you?' Marc asked.

'I don't want any.'

'Yes,' Ernestine said. 'I must pay you for helping me.'

Daniella shook her head. 'No. A few years ago somebody helped me, for nothing. Now I want to help you. Please, I'll be happy to do it; I don't want to be paid.'

Later they drove away with Ernestine's paintings on the back seat of the Mini Moke, Ernestine and Maria waving them off.

'It's fair enough to take a commission, Daniella,' Marc said as they drove out of the village. 'You're performing a service for her, it's business.' He gave her a quick, searching look.

'Not everything in life is business,' she said with a touch of impatience. 'Sometimes you just do something for somebody because you want to, not because you get something out of it.'

Their eyes met briefly and for a moment she saw in his gaze a fleeting doubt.

'Right,' he said.

They had a swim after they returned. She was aware of the change in him and the change in the atmosphere between them. His animosity seemed to have evaporated, yet she didn't feel completely at ease, conscious of another tension between them.

Going down to the beach wasn't such a brilliant idea, she admitted to herself—it was difficult to be unaffected by the stark male appeal of him. It was difficult not to look at his broad, bare chest and brown muscled legs. It was difficult to fight her feelings when she wasn't angry with him. His eyes made her uncomfortable.

As they were quietly talking she was conscious of the undercurrents between them. She was acutely aware of him, of his body, the tone of his voice, the look in his silvery eyes. And she knew, without a doubt, that he was very much aware of her as well.

They were alone on the beach, alone with the sea and the sky and the rocks, and the knowledge of their isolation heightened the sense of danger. There was no escape here. One spark could set the fires raging. It made her feel dizzy, this terrible tension, this knowing of what might happen, of what she didn't want to happen, yet did.

But nothing happened. He did not touch her, not on the beach, not in the water, and after a while they climbed the path back up to the relative safety of the house.

They had a leisurely dinner and Marc told her a joke and made her laugh. The joy of small miracles, she thought, smiling at herself.

After coffee on the veranda, Marc went inside to make some phone calls. Daniella tried to read her book, but despite the calm serenity of the warm night she felt unaccountably restless. Marc reappeared an hour later, asking if she wanted some rum punch.

'Yes, please.' Maybe it would ease the tension inside her.

'I'll be right back,' he said, and went in search of the drinks.

Not able to sit still, she got to her feet and leaned against the veranda railing, sniffing the salty tang of sea air. The boats were out again, small lights on the horizon. She scanned the sky and tried to find the constellations Marc had pointed out to her the night before. It would take some practice, she decided.

Marc came back, bringing a pitcher of rum punch and filled their glasses. He came to stand beside her and handed her a glass.

'Anything out there?' he asked.

'Stars,' she said, smiling. 'And some boats. Fishing boats, yachts, I don't know.' She sipped her drink. The ice tinkled against the glass.

'Pirates.'

She frowned. 'Pirates?'

He gave a crooked grin. 'Men with black eye-patches and wooden legs. Ships full of silver and gold and ammunition and barrels of whisky.' He made a sweeping gesture with his left hand. 'They're all around the islands here, didn't you know?' He sounded playful, which was rather surprising.

She looked at the twinkling lights out on the water. 'I didn't know. How very romantic.'

The island's history was full of colourful stories of pirates and their frightful deeds, tales of long ago, romanticised into legends, no doubt. She knew many of them, had heard them from the locals or read about them in books.

'They're waiting for just the right moment to come ashore and kidnap you,' Marc went on, his voice low and ominous.

'You're a few centuries out of date,' she whispered. She didn't know why she was whispering, but the night around them and the dark sea at the horizon seemed to create a secretive atmosphere.

'What's the matter with your imagination?' he whispered back.

There was nothing wrong with her imagination, but being kidnapped by one-eyed pirates had never been one of her fantasies. Yet now, surrounded by the mysterious darkness, on this small island, it seemed a fantasy worth pursuing.

'I'll kick and scream and then I'll faint,' she said.

He nodded his approval. 'They'll put you on board and take you to a far and foreign land and sell you to a sheikh.'

She frowned suspiciously, thinking of Simone who had predicted a trip to a far continent. 'Are you psychic?'

His laugh was soft and amused. 'Why?'

'Never mind.' She took a healthy draught of the fruity drink for fortification. Maybe Simone had seen her trip to St Barlow. Not that the tiny island could be considered a continent, but then, even psychics made mistakes.

'Don't you want to live with a romantic sheikh?' he asked.

She considered this, then wrinkled her nose. 'Not if he's old and smelly and has twenty other women in his harem!'

'Picky, picky.'

'Oh, very. So what's going to happen to poor little me?'

'You will have to be rescued, I suppose.' He frowned. 'You'll have to help me out here. I've never read that kind of novel.'

She finished her drink and smiled serenely. 'You started it, you finish it.' He got her kidnapped and sold to a sheikh, now he'd better save her. Fast. The sheikh had paid a lot of gold for her, he'd better have, and would want his money's worth. She gave a delicate little shiver—it was not a happy thought. She took the pitcher and poured herself another drink.

Marc sighed. 'Well, I suppose fair is fair. Let's see now. Maybe you don't need to be rescued after all. Maybe the sheikh is not old and smelly. Maybe you fall madly in love with him.'

She looked at him doubtfully. 'He has a shower at least once a day, and more if it's really hot.'

'OK, fine. What else?'

'No other women.'

He groaned. 'A sheikh without women: that's hard to swallow.'

She took a sip from her drink; she was very thirsty. 'Either that or I have to be rescued.'

He thought for a moment. 'All right. The sheikh is young and widowed and only you will be able to break

through his grief.' His hand touched her hair, fingers
gently lifting the curls. 'You're blonde and beautiful——' he said softly '—and the sheikh is utterly
captivated.'

She shook her head. 'I've been deflowered and defiled
by twenty pirates. No self-respecting sheikh is going to
want me.'

He groaned again. 'I need another drink.' He pushed
himself away from the railing.

She handed him her empty glass. 'Me too. I'm a
prisoner in a harem—I need all the help I can get!'

He poured the punch, then sat down on a rattan two-
seater. He patted the flowered cushion next to him. 'Sit
down.'

She did. She was enjoying the fantasy. She was feeling
relaxed now. 'I want to be rescued,' she said. 'I don't
believe in a grieving sheikh who takes showers twice a
day and I don't want to live in a desert.'

'But it would be so romantic. You will live in a casbah
full of beautiful rugs and you'll wear silk and jewels
every day. You'll eat fresh figs and dates and live a life
of leisure.'

'And grow lazy and stupid—no way! I want to be
rescued.' She took another drink from her glass. She
was beginning to feel pleasantly relaxed.

'Who's going to rescue you?'

'You. You shouldn't have let those pirates take me in
the first place. What kind of coward are you, anyway?'

He looked wounded. 'I didn't see them coming. The
phone was ringing and I had to go inside.'

She choked on the punch. She coughed and spluttered
and he slapped her back. Tears were streaming down her
cheeks; he handed her a paper napkin and she wiped
her eyes.

'Sorry,' he said, leaving his hand on her back, stroking
it.

'Me too.' She took a deep breath. 'I'm stuck in the desert with a smelly sheikh and you won't rescue me.'

'I'll come and rescue you,' he said in a soothing tone.

'Really?'

He nodded gravely. 'But it may take a while. I'll have to take evening classes in how to ride a camel first!'

'Of course,' she murmured.

'Will you be able to wait until I come?'

'Yes.' For him, she could wait forever. What choice did she have?

'You're very tough.'

'Yes, I know.' She sighed. 'Sometimes I get really tired of being tough.'

'Why is that?'

'Because it's tiring.' She leaned her head against his shoulder and closed her eyes; she felt a little drowsy. It was a nice feeling.

'Of course, that makes sense.' He put his arm around her. 'After I rescue you, you won't have to be tough any more. I'll defy hunger, thirst and all the perils of the desert and find you. I'll poison everybody in the casbah and come to your room in the dead of night. How am I doing so far?'

'Sounds nice,' she murmured.

'Will you be happy to see me?'

She nodded. He pulled her a little closer and she rubbed her cheek against the smooth cotton of his shirt. She rested her hand on his chest; she could feel the solid thudding of his heart under her fingers. It felt good and comfortable.

It felt more than comfortable. Somewhere in the far recess of her mind she knew something wasn't quite right. She couldn't think what it was, so she pushed the thought away. A velvety breeze touched her face. She opened her eyes and glanced up at the sky which was very dark and full of stars. It was a magical night. She smiled, then turned to look at Marc. His face was very close, her cheek touching his. She felt warm and light-headed. She wanted him to kiss her.

'Marc?'

'Yes?' His voice was very low.

'Have you ever made love in the desert?'

He chuckled. 'No.' He turned his head slightly, his lips brushing against her mouth and her pulse leaped.

Kiss me, she said silently, kiss me.

His eyes held hers and there was no way she could look away. She was transfixed by the emotion in his eyes, the smouldering desire, then suddenly it was gone, as if a light inside him had been switched off.

He released her slowly, reluctantly. 'It's hard work rescuing a woman from a casbah,' he said evenly. 'I'd better catch up on my rest.' He stood up, pulling her with him by the hand. 'Come on. Time for bed.' With his arm around her, he led her back into the house, to her room. At the door, he kissed her gently. 'Goodnight, Daniella. Don't dream of the sheikh.' He opened the door across the hall from hers and went inside.

Please, she wanted to say, please stay with me. I need you. But the words didn't come and she moved into her room, feeling bereft and lonely.

She got ready for bed and slipped between the cool cotton sheets, her limbs heavy and tired. She let out a deep sigh, feeling her body grow weightless.

Images of men and camels and sun-baked desert danced through her dreams. The sheikh was old and mean and beat her with a belt, telling her she was a worthless creature, a bastard child nobody wanted. He looked like her grandfather. Every night she stood at the small barred window of her room at the casbah and looked at the sky, seeing eternity, far and unreachable.

She would run away a soon as she had found the sheikh's pay cheque and his antique watch. He was hiding them from her. Peanut butter sandwiches were a problem. There was no peanut butter anywhere in the casbah.

Then one night as she stood at her window, searching the cold desert sky for the constellations, she saw something moving in the dark. A man in flowing robes, eerie in the moonlight, floated towards the casbah on a camel. He came closer and closer, then moved past her window. For one heart-stopping moment, their eyes made contact. She saw his face, the pale silver eyes, and she knew who had come to rescue her.

In a secret part of her heart she had always known he would come to rescue her.

She wanted to call out, but her mouth was dry and no sound came. He disappeared into the night and she stood in front of the window and waited, trembling. A great wind began to blow across the desert, stirring up clouds of swirling sand. She hugged herself and shivered.

He didn't come. For a long time she listened to the wind howling around the casbah and still he didn't come. She wanted to search for him, but her room was locked at night and she could not get out. Fear engulfed her. What if something had happened to Marc?

Finally the door opened and he was there, resplendent in his white robes, grinning triumphantly. Her heart began to beat rapidly and as he enfolded her into his embrace, she felt her body weaken with love and desire.

She woke up. The room was dark and she was clutching the pillow to her chest. Her heart was racing. She heard the crashing of the waves on the beach, loud, too loud. Wind lashed the palm trees, blew in through the open window and across her body. She was alone in the dark. Curling herself into a ball, she buried her face in the pillow and closed her eyes tightly.

But all she saw was Marc's face. He was in the other room. She would have to go to him; she couldn't stay here any longer alone in this dark room with the eerie sound of the wind and the waves. She wanted him with her.

She slipped out of her room and into his across the hall, his door creaking softly as she opened it. A narrow crack in the curtains let in some faint moonlight and she vaguely discerned Marc's dark shape on the big bed. He was lying on his back, a sheet pulled halfway across his bare chest. One arm lay by his side, the other across his stomach. His breathing was slow and regular.

Without making a sound she moved forward and slipped next to him under the sheet, her body tingling with nerves. She shifted closer to his side, feeling the warmth of his sleeping body through her thin nightgown.

'Marc?' she whispered.

He made an unintelligible sound and turned on his side, facing her. His arm went around her and drew her close against him, yet he went on sleeping. He was naked under the sheet and her body tingled with awareness. A dangerous headiness took hold of her. Her face was almost touching his and his breath feathered along her cheek. She was overwhelmed with longing—sweet, painful longing that made her breathing shallow and her body warm with desire. She brushed her mouth against his lips and he stirred again, emitting a soft groan deep in his throat.

'Daniella?' he muttered sleepily.

'I'm here.'

'Mmmm...' One hand slid along her back, over her hip and thigh, then back up over her stomach to her breast. On and on his hand moved over her body, touching and searching and caressing and fire raced through her. Finally he let out a deep sigh and opened his eyes.

'Daniella?' he asked again, as if he wasn't sure she was really there, as if afraid he'd only been dreaming.

'Yes. I...I was dreaming. There's a storm. I didn't want to be alone.'

His arms locked her against him. 'Oh, Daniella,' he said huskily.

'I waited for you so long,' she whispered and suddenly her eyes were full of tears and she began to cry. A sadness, deep and vast, pressed on her heart. 'You didn't come and I...'

'Ssh,' he said softly, stroking her face. 'It's all right. I'm here now.'

'Hold me, oh, Marc, please hold me.' She wasn't sure why she was crying, why this vast, aching sadness overwhelmed her so completely, so suddenly.

'I'm holding you.' His mouth brushed her lips. 'I'm holding you.'

CHAPTER NINE

DANIELLA pressed her face against Marc's bare chest, feeling the wetness of her own tears. His skin was warm and she could hear the solid thudding of his heart.

'I'm scared,' she said.

'Why?' He stroked her hair, softly, sensuously.

'I don't know.' Was it the dream? Or fear of the mysterious sadness that a moment ago had filled her heart and mind? Or was it the wind in the palms and the crashing of the waves on the beach?

'Did the wind wake you up?' he asked.

'Yes... and the dream.' It seemed very real still, and she shivered as the images leaped into her mind. 'I was waiting for you to come. I was in a room with bars in front of the windows and I couldn't get out. There was a sandstorm. It was awful.'

'It was only a dream.' He dropped soothing little kisses on her forehead. His hand moved under her nightgown, stroking her thigh and hip. His touch chased away the clouds in her mind and she took a deep, shuddering breath. It felt good, so good, to be here in his arms. She kissed his chest, the dark mat of curly hair tickling her lips. The fear flowed out of her as her body filled with sweet desire.

She sighed. 'And this, is this a dream too?'

'No,' he said huskily, 'this is not a dream.' He lifted her face and kissed her, his mouth urgent and eager.

But of course this had to be a dream. It had to be a dream to be in his arms, to feel her whole body come alive under his touch.

'Marc,' she whispered, 'I want you so much, so much...I don't know...I don't understand——'

'Ssh.' He put a finger on her mouth. 'I want you too.' He pushed the thin straps of her nightgown aside, freeing her breasts, kissing first one nipple, then the other, and she felt a delicious tingling pain spiralling all through her.

'Oh...' she breathed.

He laughed softly. 'You like that?'

'Yes.'

The caress of his hand was silky soft, the pleasure of his touch like food for her starved senses. She could not get enough of it; she could not get enough of him. She felt as if she were drowning and she clung to him, mindless, holding on to him tightly.

'Relax,' he said, humour in his voice. 'I'm not leaving.'

'Make love to me, Marc, please...'

'I'm trying to,' he said, amusement spilling over in his voice. 'Let's get rid of this thing you're wearing.' He tugged at her nightgown and proceeded to slip it off over her head.

The windows were open and she heard the sound of the wind in the palm trees, the waves rolling ashore, crashing on to the beach. Over and over and over and over. She could feel the tension in the air, the brewing of a storm, mirroring the build-up of tension in herself.

Then all the slow, sleepy movements were gone and a wild passion took over. His mouth and hands searched her body, caressing, kissing, tasting, setting her on fire. Her senses singing, she responded with all the need and yearning she'd restrained for too long, loving him, loving his body. It was a feverish, urgent lovemaking, speaking of all the lonely years of silent desire and secret dreams.

Outside the storm broke loose, as did the storm in their fevered bodies with magic perfection. Sated and breathless, she heard the rain come pouring from the heavens and she smiled in the dark, her heart overflowing.

Their bodies stilled against each other and she revelled in the sensation of drowsy languor that overtook her. He did not let her go; he held her close, one hand resting on her breast, his breath fanning her cheek. There was no more talking, as if their voices would break the secret magic of the night. She listened to the rain drenching the trees and bushes, soaking the earth. After a while the rain slowed down, as did her heartbeat, and she fell asleep in his arms hearing only the soft dripping on the foliage outside the window.

Daniella drifted back to consciousness with the sunlight streaming over her face, and the sound of joyous bird song dancing in on the breeze through the open window. For a moment, she luxuriated in the lazy, languorous feel of her body as it was slowly coming to life. Then suddenly she was fully awake as she became aware of Marc's body next to her in bed and Marc's eyes watching her with a silvery shine of amusement.

'Good morning,' he said.

She could not speak; she could only look at him as memory washed over her and the knowledge that what had happened was not a dream but reality. There was the awful feeling that she didn't know if she was happy or horrified or both.

'Something wrong?' he asked.

She shook her head. 'I don't know.' Her voice sounded odd, not at all like her own. She needed to think. She lay back and closed her eyes, trying to remember how she had ended up in this bed. Images flashed through her befuddled mind and it took a moment to grasp their significance: pirates, a sheikh, a barred window, Marc on a camel.

She pushed her face in her pillow and moaned. They'd been fantasising, making up a ridiculous story. She'd been drinking rum punch. Too much rum punch! Then later, alone in bed, the dream had finished her. She'd felt lonely and sad and she'd left her room and gone to Marc.

She moaned again. It had been a mistake! Nothing had changed, nothing had been resolved. Sex never did resolve anything. Sex didn't solve problems—love did.

And this had not been love.

How could she have been so stupid?

His hand laced through her hair and his mouth was close to her ear. 'It's all right,' he whispered. 'It's all right, Daniella.'

She moved away from his touch; she didn't want him touching her just now. 'I'm sorry,' she said, her voice choking. She sat up, turning her face away, helpless despair suffusing her.

Her eyes caught sight of the little box on the bedside table. It took a moment before she realised what it was. Her heart began to pound—a heavy, painful thundering against her ribs.

Last night had not been a foolish mistake.

One way or another Marc had planned it to happen. He had *planned* to make love to her. Proof was right there on the bedside table. Maybe that was why he had come to the island—to seduce her.

He reached for her hand. 'Daniella, come here.'

She froze, yanking her hand free. 'No.' She looked at him, hating him.

He sat up. Tousled hair hung over his forehead. He frowned, confusion on his face. 'What's wrong?'

She glared at him, shaking. 'What's wrong? How dare you even ask? Everything is wrong!' Tears stung her eyes. 'You planned this,' she choked. 'It wasn't just a simple, stupid mistake because I had one too many rum punches!'

He dragged his fingers through his hair. 'I didn't plan it, Daniella.'

'Oh, come on! Then why this?' She picked up the little box and threw it across the room. 'You always keep these handy? You carry them around in your wallet?'

'I bought them yesterday morning.'

'And that's not premeditation?'

'I'd call it being sensible, being realistic. I've never yet heard of a woman blaming a man for thinking of contraception.'

'I'd like to know why you went out to buy them if you weren't planning to get me into bed. You explain that to me!'

'Because I wanted you. Because of what was going on between us. Because I knew that something might happen I had no control over and I had enough guts to admit it to myself. And I was damned right.' His eyes held hers. 'You came to me, Daniella, not the other way around.'

'I had three drinks. I'm not used to a lot of——'

'I didn't make you drink them,' he said quietly. 'Maybe it was what you needed to cut down all those defences and admit to yourself that you wanted me.'

'Well, I hope you're happy!' She searched the floor and the bed for her nightgown. She had to get away, away from him, away from the island.

He sighed heavily. 'No, not particularly.' He hesitated for a moment. 'Daniella, I heard you cry the other night.'

Her heart turned over and her hand stilled, crumpling the sheet in her fingers. 'I don't know what you mean.'

He searched her face. 'Yes, you do. You were crying and it took all my strength not to get up and go to you. I knew well enough what would happen if I did.'

'You're such a gentleman,' she said, but her voice sounded thick and failed to produce the mocking tone she had intended. She looked under the sheet, finally discovering her nightgown, crumpled at the bottom of the bed.

'Why were you crying, Daniella?'

Tears of humiliation clouded her eyes. She dragged on the wrinkled nightgown and crawled out of bed. 'I can't imagine why you'd care.' She stood by the bed and glared at him. 'And if you're still thinking I'll leave your father's house because of *you*, you're sadly mistaken!'

His eyes held hers, but she saw only a dull weariness.

'Stay,' he said tonelessly. 'Stay, if that's what you want.'

'*Thank you!*' she said caustically. She swung around and fled out of the room.

She left the island the same day and stayed with Anne for a couple of days before returning home on Saturday. She was accompanying Hayden to a glamorous charity ball that evening and she had to go back sooner or later anyway.

Mrs Bell told her Marc had come home the night before but had gone out for the day with Gregory. She wasn't sure when he'd be back. Late, Daniella hoped. The few days she'd spent at Anne's had given her some much-needed space, but she'd just as soon not face Marc if she didn't have to.

She took her time getting ready for the ball—she had a leisurely bath, shampooed her hair and painted her toe and finger nails. Dressed in a long evening gown of shimmering blue silk, she went down to the library to tell Hayden she was ready to go. But when she opened the door, it wasn't Hayden she found, but Marc. Wearing faded blue jeans and a striped T-shirt, he sat in a chair, a stack of paper—some sort of document—on his thighs.

He stared at her wordlessly for a long moment, and she felt the heat rise into her cheeks. Her mouth went dry and she was incapable of averting her gaze. She tried to read his expression, but there was nothing, nothing. Eyes grey and remote. Eyes like a barren wasteland.

'Hello, Daniella,' he said calmly. 'You look very beautiful.'

'Thank you.'

'My father will be right back. Would you like me to pour you a drink?'

She tensed. 'No, thank you.' The last time she'd had a drink with him... Why did she feel like crying? Like hitting him, hurting him? He wasn't worth all these emotions he stirred up inside her. She felt degraded, humiliated. She'd let herself be swept away by his love-making, by the tenderness in his hands and eyes. Whom had he seen when he was making love to her? The girl she'd been three years ago? Certainly not the woman he thought she was now, the woman in her evening gown ready to go out with his wealthy old father.

She was about to turn around and leave the room when Hayden came in. He looked magnificent in his black evening clothes—tall and energetic, his grey hair gleaming in the lamp light. His brown eyes smiling, he gave her a look of warm appraisal.

'Beautiful,' he said. He took her hand and tucked her arm through his. 'Let's go.'

She moved through the evening like an automaton, smiling and talking at all the appropriate times, her mind in turmoil. Marc wasn't leaving for another month or so. If only she could get away. But there was no way out. With the group show coming up at the Benedict in a couple of weeks, she could not possibly leave, there was no escape. She didn't know how she was going to make it through the coming month.

On Monday she was having lunch with Jade. It was a sunny May day and they were seated in a small courtyard at the back of the main restaurant: a secluded, idyllic place with small tables and flowering potted plants. It looked very European, quiet and peaceful. They were seated at a table with a blue and white tablecloth and flowered French country dishes.

'This is lovely,' Daniella sighed. 'Where did you find this place?'

'I know the owner.' Jade laughed, tossing her black hair back over her shoulder. 'Don't tell anyone about it. It's my secret hide-out and I don't want it overrun by yuppy lawyers.'

Daniella smiled. 'My lips are sealed.'

The food was delicious, and as always Daniella enjoyed Jade's company, yet she was distracted and found it hard to keep up with Jade's stories.

'What's wrong?' Jade asked her at last. 'You're very quiet.'

Daniella sighed. 'Sorry. I'm lousy company.'

Jade gave her a penetrating look. 'It's Marc, isn't it? I'm sorry I asked him to the party, but I had no idea...' Jade made a helpless gesture with her hand, her words trailing away into silence.

Daniella managed a smile. 'It was your party; you were free to invite whomever you wanted.' She'd forgotten about the party. All she could think of was the time they'd spent on St Barlow, thinking and analysing and trying to make sense out of it.

Jade grimaced. 'And then Clarissa showed up. Bad news, that.' She gave Daniella a searching look. 'You know about Marc and Clarissa, I assume?'

'Not much. She dropped him because she didn't want to go to Peru with him.'

Jade nodded. 'A real sweetheart, that one.'

'Would you go?'

'Would I go where? To South America?' Jade laughed. 'With my Charlie I'd go anywhere: Antarctica, Papua New Guinea. You name it.'

Daniella smiled, feeling a twinge of envy. 'With Charlie being a congressional reporter, you won't have to worry too much.'

'No, not too much.' Jade sipped her wine. 'With Marc, of course, it's another story. Clarissa should have known from the beginning he wasn't going to stick around here.'

'How long did they know each other?'

'Well over two years, I think. He was travelling a lot in that time, and he'd spent several years overseas before they met. Surely it wasn't a surprise he was going to Peru?' Jade sipped her wine, frowning a little as if contemplating the wisdom of telling the story.

Daniella stared at her plate. She wasn't sure if she wanted to know more about their relationship; she wasn't sure she cared.

Jade straightened in her seat. 'Clarissa didn't want to go to South America, but that wasn't all.' She wiped her mouth with her napkin and put it back in her lap. 'She dumped him because Marc refused to join his father's company. She'd hoped she'd be able to change his mind about that. She had her heart set on being the new "mistress of the mansion", so to speak.' Jade made a face. 'She's quite the social climber, our Clarissa. And in case you wonder—no, I didn't invite her personally.

Somebody brought her; I do not count her among my friends.'

'Phew, that's a relief.' Daniella looked at Jade and frowned. 'Why did Marc fall for her? Surely he could see past that beautiful exterior after a couple of weeks?'

Jade laughed. 'Love. It makes people blind and deaf and stupid. Especially men.'

Daniella bit her lip. She'd thought those very same things about Marc, that he was blind and deaf. She kept asking herself why he was that way and could find no answer. Not because of love at any rate, that was clear enough.

'Clarissa took whatever she could get out of him, and that was considerable,' Jade went on. 'Marc's a generous man and she took advantage of it in the most blatant way. He gave her big, expensive presents and took her on trips to Europe and the Far East, but it was never enough. I know because I've heard her talk. She always wanted more. For some reason I'll never understand, she thought he owed it to her. He gave her a new car for her birthday three days before she dumped him. She didn't give it back; she's greedy enough to have timed it perfectly.'

Daniella had a sick feeling in the pit of her stomach. She put down her fork and slowly sipped her mineral water. She saw again in her mind the beautiful face, the petulant mouth. 'What is she doing now? I mean, does she have someone else? Is she married?'

'Oh, she's married all right. Didn't take her long, either; about two months after she dropped Marc she found this old geezer who made his fortune in pet food. He's well into his seventies now and—are you all right?'

Daniella wiped her mouth with her napkin. Her hand trembled and her stomach churned. 'I'm all right,' she lied, taking another drink of water.

'You look like death.' Jade's voice was low and astonished. 'What did I say? I just thought...'

Daniella took a deep breath and gave a quavering smile. 'Nothing, nothing. I'm all right, Jade, really.' She swallowed and pushed her plate away. 'I think I'm done with this. Let's have some espresso.'

The waiter brought their coffee and the subject was changed. Jade invited her to spend a weekend at her beach house on the Maryland coast. 'I know it's early in the season, but I need to get out of town,' she said.

'Thanks, I'd love to.' Getting out of town was a wonderful idea.

'Bring your paints,' Jade suggested.

'Oh, I will.'

On the way home Daniella thought about Clarissa and the things Jade had told her. It didn't surprise her any more why Marc thought she too was a fortune-hunter. All she felt was a hopeless sense of desolation and a deep, dull ache in the region of her heart.

Andrew was invited to the beach as well, and he offered to take Daniella so they didn't have to make the long drive by themselves in separate cars. He drove up to the house at six on Friday afternoon. Carrying her small overnight suitcase, Daniella left the house and closed the door behind her. Marc was shooting baskets with Gregory and he looked up briefly as she walked up to Andrew's car.

There was an odd look on Marc's face—a look she didn't dare interpret. It was obvious what he was thinking, and she cursed herself for not having more sense than to have Andrew come to the house to pick her up. For a crazy moment, she wanted to stop right there, in the driveway, and explain to Marc that she was not going out with Andrew on a cosy hideaway weekend in the country while Hayden was in New Orleans.

Of course it would be useless. Also, she wasn't guilty, so why should she defend herself?

Marc had not been around much the past week, and neither had Hayden, but the few times they had been together at meals had been nerve-racking, at least for her. Outwardly, everything seemed to be quite normal. She was good at pretending nothing was wrong, making casual conversation, but she hadn't been able to feel cool and indifferent inside. Every time she looked at Marc, her heart would ache. Every time she watched his lean fingers, she longed to be touched again.

She climbed into the car and waved out of the window. 'I'll see you Sunday,' she said lightly.

'Have a good time,' he said, but his tone of voice mocked her.

She sat back in the seat and sighed, feeling a sense of hopelessness like a cloud gathering over the day.

'What's wrong?' Andrew asked, frowning at her.

She shook her head. 'Nothing.'

He asked no further, much to her relief. After an hour they stopped for dinner in a restaurant just off the main road, a family-run affair that served good, hearty food, and Daniella found her appetite and managed to tuck away a fair meal.

'Feeling better?' Andrew asked.

'Much, thanks.' She wasn't going to let her thoughts of Marc ruin her weekend. Also, she was not going to discuss it with Andrew. She eyed the dessert tray. 'They've got homemade strawberry shortcake. How about it, shall we have some?'

He gave a crooked smile. 'Sure, why not?'

It was a long drive to the beach and it was late when they arrived. The house was large and built on stilts, the weathered wood giving it a rustic look. A fire had been built in the spacious living-room and the other guests— a couple and two singles—were already there, sipping wine and eating snacks. Except for one of the women, Daniella knew everybody and despite her fatigue she joined them in front of the fire and spent another hour talking before she went to bed.

She awoke early the next morning, slipped carefully out of the quiet house and went for a long walk along the beach. It was only May and the breeze felt cool and fresh. She took off her sneakers and waded into the water, but only for a minute; the water was still freezing. How different this was from the warm turquoise waters of St Barlow!

Don't think about St Barlow. Don't think about Marc.

When she got back, people had congregated in the kitchen, drinking coffee and eating the croissants and sweet rolls someone had picked up at the local bakery. Andrew pulled out a chair for her and gave her a cup of coffee. It was strong and hot and tasted delicious after her walk. She took one of the sweet rolls and slathered butter on it—she was suddenly ravenous.

The phone rang and Jade went to answer it, coming back a minute later with the laughter erased from her face.

'What's wrong?' Andrew asked.

'Daniella, it's for you.'

Daniella jumped to her feet, alarmed. 'What's the matter?'

'It's Mrs Bell. There was a fire at the house last night.'

'A fire?' Hot fear rushed through her blood. She ran into the hall and grabbed the phone. 'Mrs Bell?' she almost shouted. 'Where's Hayden? What happened? Didn't the alarms go off?'

'Calm down, child,' Mrs Bell's voice came over the line. 'Mr Penbrooke wasn't there—Hayden, that is. And the alarms worked just fine, except nobody was home to hear them. Not until Marc came home, that is. He found the place in flames and that stupid boy went inside and——'

'Inside? Oh, my God, was Hayden——'

'Hayden wasn't there, I told you, child. He's in New Orleans.'

Yes, of course. She wiped the hair out of her face. She couldn't think. She took a deep breath. 'But...I...Marc knew I wasn't home. Why then...?'

'He went in to get your paintings.'

She felt her heart sink. Her paintings for the show. Marc. Marc in the middle of a burning house. She closed her eyes, trying to shut off the vision, but it was still there behind her eyelids.

Her whole body began to shake. 'What happened? Is he all right?'

'He's in the hospital. He...'

It was as if someone was squeezing her heart. 'No,' she said, her voice so low she hardly recognised it herself. 'Oh, no!'

'He'll be all right, child. Calm down, please. He'll be all right.'

Her legs wouldn't hold her up any more. Her back slid down the wall until she sat on the floor, hugging her knees into her chest.

She barely heard the rest of Mrs Bell's explanations. Something about faulty wiring in the wall outside her studio, about the damage not being too bad, about all her paintings being rescued.

He's crazy, she said to herself, repeating it over and over again. He'd gone into a burning house to rescue her paintings and now he was in the hospital, hurt, in pain.

'I'm coming home.' She glanced at her watch. 'I'll be back some time this afternoon.' Maybe she could borrow Andrew's car and he could get a ride back to Washington with someone else tomorrow.

But Andrew wouldn't hear of it. He would drive her home; she was in no state to drive herself.

'I'm OK,' she said. 'Really. Please, Andrew, I don't want to ruin your weekend.'

'I'm driving,' he said, and that was the end of it.

All the way home she thought of Marc, seeing terrible visions of arms and legs swathed in bandages. Her throat ached. Was Mrs Bell telling the truth? Was he really all right? And what was *all right*? How badly was he hurt?

Why was she feeling this terrible pain and worry? Oh, don't be stupid, she told herself. You know why. You love him. Despite everything, you still love him. You're stupid and crazy and you love him.

Please, she prayed, don't let him be hurt.

CHAPTER TEN

HER heart beat far too wildly as she walked through the long hospital corridors to Marc's room, late that afternoon. The air smelled stuffy and stale.

He sat up in bed, reading a book. For a moment she just stood in the door and watched him, her heart in her throat. No bandages, no machines, only nose-tubes leading to an oxygen outlet in the wall. He looked perfectly normal, but out of place in this room. He didn't look sick—he looked vitally, gloriously alive. She fought the impulse to run up to him, throw her arms around him and press her face against his chest. He glanced up, his eyes meeting hers. Her heart turned over and she advanced into the room.

'You're not burned.' Her voice was low and unsteady and she fought the tears of relief stinging her eyes.

'Just some smoke-inhalation.' He frowned. 'What are you doing here? I thought you were out with Andrew.'

She swallowed and wiped her clammy hands on her jeans. 'I wasn't out with him. I was at Jade's beach house. Mrs Bell called me. I came back to see you.'

'That wasn't necessary,' he said evenly, as if speaking to a stranger.

'Yes it was. It is. How are you feeling?'

'Fine. Just a bit tight in the chest. They've taken some X-rays and I'm having some oxygen. I'll be home tomorrow.'

Relief made her almost giddy. He wasn't burned, he wasn't dying. Then worry changed into anger; her hands clenched into fists. 'You shouldn't have done it. You

155

were stupid and reckless and an idiot to do what you did.'

'Thank you,' he said drily. 'You make my day.'

She stood next to the bed, clasping and unclasping her hands, fighting tears. 'You could have killed yourself, don't you know that?'

'No, I couldn't. I'm not stupid.'

She plunked herself inelegantly in a chair. 'Yes, you are.'

He raised a sardonic eyebrow. 'I thought you might like your paintings saved.'

She closed her eyes briefly. 'Of course I do, Marc. My paintings mean a lot to me, and with a show coming up, I . . . but for you to risk your *life* . . . why did you do it?'

He shrugged. 'Art can't be replaced.'

She stared at him. 'They're only paintings.' Compared to someone's life, the importance of her paintings seemed insignificant.

'No, they're not. They're *your* paintings. And they're good and I didn't want them destroyed.'

She swallowed at the constriction in her throat. 'How did you even know they were good? You've never seen them.'

His mouth quirked. 'Oh, I knew they were good. One day, when you weren't home, I went into your studio to look at them.'

Something stirred in her mind, a memory. The mystery of the unlocked doors of her studio was solved now. 'Oh, I see.' He had invaded her privacy, intruded into the place no one else entered without her permission, but it seemed hardly worth getting upset about under the circumstances.

She felt her throat close, tears welling up in her eyes. A lump of pain and regret lodged in her throat. He loves me, she thought, but he'll never admit it. No matter what he says, he did it because he loves me, but not the me he thinks I am. He's in love with the girl who paints the pictures.

But to him, the girl who painted the pictures was only an illusion. The real person was the girl who'd seduced his father and lived off his money and went out with other men. Somehow the two conflicting images were not to be reconciled in his mind.

She stared out of the window, trying to control her tears. She swallowed at the lump in her throat. 'I don't know how to thank you,' she said after a while.

'I don't need your thanks,' he said coolly, and she felt as if he'd slapped her in the face.

'You're mad at me,' she stated.

'I'm not mad at you.'

'Oh, but you are. It's because of Andrew, isn't it? You don't like me going out with him or doing anything with him.'

He shrugged. 'Why shouldn't I?'

'You tell me! Andrew is my friend; I am not in love with him; I'm not having an affair with him or ever have, for that matter. I told you this before. Not that it's any of your damn business!' She swallowed, feeling like a fool. She was defending herself against accusations he hadn't made, not in words. Yet she could feel them hanging in the air between them, as clear as if they'd been spoken. 'I don't know why I'm even telling you this.'

He didn't reply and the silence stretched. She rose to her feet, her body tense and stiff. 'I'll go now. Is there anything you need?'

'No, thank you.' His expression was smooth and indifferent, and he looked at her with the eyes of a stranger.

She took a deep breath. 'Thank you for what you did. I'm glad you didn't get hurt.' It sounded hopelessly inadequate. She moved out of the door before he could answer.

He came home late the next morning and for the next few days they managed to avoid each other completely. Daniella walked around in a daze, a lump of misery like a rock in her stomach. There was a momentary joy when she received news that one of Ernestine's paintings had been sold—a ray of sunshine in the gloom of her days.

She'd moved into another room in the house while a crew of workmen undertook repairs on her room, the studio and the hall outside. The mess was a shock, but she had no energy to worry about the loss of her things. Her clothes had escaped the fire but the smoke and the water had created a lot of damage. She'd have to go out and buy more clothes.

I could tell him I'll leave, she thought, crazed by a sudden terror. If it would make him happy, I'll leave. But of course she did not. Always she would come to her senses. He wouldn't tell her he loved her just because she'd left his father's house. He would never admit to it as long as he believed she was taking advantage of his father.

I'll go to Hayden and tell him everything, she thought frantically. I'll tell him to please explain to Marc what is or is not going on. But she could not do that either. Hayden would never forgive his son.

Daniella had been to a lot of openings and other fancy gatherings, but the opening of the group show was different. She was nervous, as were the other two artists taking part in the exhibit. She kept wringing her hands, sighing, adjusting her hair, much to Anne's amusement.

'I didn't know you had it in you,' she said. 'You're always so cool and collected.'

'I'm cool and collected now,' Daniella said, squaring her shoulders and lifting her chin.

'Sure you are.'

'I don't care if people don't show up,' she declared with a great show of bravado. 'I don't care if my paintings don't sell.' She tore at her hair and groaned. 'Oh, God, I'm going to die.'

'No, you are not. You're going to drink champagne and smile and make intelligent conversation and listen to what they have to say.'

'They're going to tear everything apart.'

She felt an arm around her shoulder. 'No, they're not,' came Andrew's voice. He propelled her away, into his office, where he took her in his arms and kissed her avidly.

'This is for good luck,' he said as he withdrew. He smiled into her eyes. 'Don't worry,' he said reassuringly. 'Everything will be fine. I have great confidence in you.'

She sighed and leaned into him, her head on his shoulder. 'Thank you. You're nice to me.'

And he was. Andrew was nice. He was a friend and she could always count on him. He understood art. He was also handsome and available and so why couldn't she just be in love with him? It would be a perfect match.

No, it wouldn't. He didn't fit the picture she had in her head, the picture of a family with children. She couldn't see Andrew getting up at the ungodly hour of five o'clock on a misty spring morning to go fishing with his kids. Andrew liked his creature comforts too much. She couldn't visualise him helping his children with their science projects, or even shooting baskets for an hour or so. Perhaps she wasn't being fair. Once he was a father, maybe he would grow into these things ... No, not Andrew. He was too much of a selfish hedonist, too busy partying and wining and dining and doing his own things.

'Of course I'm nice to you,' Andrew said. 'You're my favourite artist and I love you.'

'That's what you tell yourself.' She didn't believe he really loved her.

'I've known you for three years. Do you suppose I don't know?'

She smiled. 'You're seriously deluded.'

'I want to marry you.'

'Why?'

'So I can sleep with you.'

'I was afraid of that. That's the worst reason I've ever heard.'

'What's wrong with sleeping together?' He looked wounded.

'Nothing. Oh, please, stop it, Andrew. Let's get back. Pour me some champagne.'

There wasn't time to be nervous for long—there were too many visitors demanding her attention. It pleased her to be able to talk about her own paintings; she revelled in the attention and the positive comments she heard about her work.

Hayden had promised to come and she kept an eye out for him, spotting him at last accompanied by Marc. Her mouth went dry. She had not expected Marc to come.

After they'd greeted her briefly, they made the rounds, scrutinising the art work displayed in the various rooms. Later she saw Marc speaking to Andrew and, with an odd premonition, she watched the two disappear into Andrew's office. She didn't know how long they were there or when Marc left, because for the next hour or so she was busy talking with the gallery visitors. She managed, somehow, to push the fear back in her mind and not let it take over as she was talking with the guests.

She didn't see Marc again. After the closing, Andrew took her, Anne and the other artists out to dinner to celebrate. He was pleased with the turn-out for the opening. She wanted to ask him what he and Marc had been discussing in the office, but she didn't want to do it in the presence of the others and there was no other opportunity to speak to him alone that evening.

It was after one when she finally made it home. She tiptoed up the stairs, trying to make as little noise as possible. The light in Marc's room was still on and she crept past it hoping he wouldn't hear her.

No such luck. The door swung open and Marc, dressed now in jeans and a T-shirt, stood in the door.

'Did you go out celebrating?' he asked.

'Yes. Andrew was very pleased with the turn-out.' Why was she so nervous? Maybe she was just tired.

'It was very impressive,' he said. 'Your paintings are beautiful and disturbing. I wanted to congratulate you. You'll do well.'

Praise from Marc. Why didn't it please her more? Maybe because he sounded so dutiful, as if it were merely an assignment to deliver the words he had spoken.

'Thank you,' she said politely, feeling depressed. She threaded a tired hand through her hair. 'I'd better get to bed. It's late.'

Marc crossed his arms in front of his chest and shifted his weight to his other foot. 'He says he loves you and wants to marry you.'

She tensed. So *she'd* been the topic of discussion in Andrew's office. 'Yes,' she said lightly.

'Will you?'

'Marry Andrew? No.'

'Why not? Not enough money?' His voice was coolly mocking.

She closed her eyes, a sinking feeling of despair settling in her heart. 'No——' she said wearily '—money doesn't enter into it.'

'Then what does?'

'Love. I don't love him. He's a friend and I like him, but it stops there.'

His eyes narrowed with calculation. 'He could be very useful to your career as an artist, especially if you marry him.'

Was he trying another angle? Trying to get rid of her by getting her to marry Andrew? She sighed. She was too tired to think. Her feet hurt. She wanted to go to bed. 'The price is too high,' she said. 'My career, nothing at all is worth living without love. Believe me, I know. Now please excuse me, I'm going to bed.'

He didn't detain her and she moved down the carpeted hall to her room. It was a good thing she was so exhausted; she fell asleep almost immediately.

Andrew was right—the exhibition was a success. There was a write-up in the paper with the most glowing critique of her work. Phrases like 'promising young talent', 'striking and provocative images', 'rare individuality'.

By the end of the first week half her paintings had been sold.

It was a dream come true.

Yet she lay in bed at night, feeling lonely, knowing that no amount of success would ever fill the aching emptiness she felt inside.

She was lucky, she told herself. She had a good life. She had Hayden, friends, her art, her job. She could make it on her own. She had a future as an artist. But she needed love. Someone just for herself, someone to love and trust; someone to share her life and dreams and hopes.

Marc was due to leave for Africa on Thursday. Wednesday approached and she had barely spoken to him—nothing more than a polite good morning and goodnight. The situation between Hayden and Marc had not improved and the tension in the house was electric. Daniella felt helpless to do anything about it.

When Marc didn't show up at dinner, she went to find him in his room. She knocked on the door.

'Come in.'

She opened the door. He was bare-chested, wearing only a faded pair of jeans. His hair was damp and the smell of soap floated in from the open bathroom door. A suitcase lay open on the bed, packed. He was folding a shirt, his eyebrows lifting in surprise when he saw her.

'I wanted to say goodbye,' she said, trying not to stare at his chest, the dark curly hair, the flat, brown stomach. 'And wish you good luck.'

'Why would you want to do that?' His tone was carefully bland.

'It's the polite thing to do, isn't it?' She swallowed hard. 'I've barely seen you since you came back from the hospital.'

'I was busy.'

'I know.' She bit her lip, wondering why this was so difficult. 'How's everything between you and your father?'

'Does it matter?'

'Of course it matters,' she said quietly. 'He's your father and you treat him as if he's a stranger.'

'Has it occurred to you that maybe he is?'

'He's your father!'

He shrugged. 'I don't see why all this matters to you.'

'Because I care about him!'

She saw his jaw harden. His teeth clamped together and he went on folding another shirt without saying a word.

The old anger came rushing back. She moved a couple of steps closer. 'What's so terrible about that?' she demanded. 'What is so strange or depraved about my caring for your father? He is almost seventy years old and he needs a little love and care, and he certainly isn't getting it from his own son!'

One eyebrow cocked sardonically. 'Spare me the lecture, will you? My dear father is a stubborn old goat who won't listen to reason. He's a nice old guy whenever things go according to his wishes, but don't get in his way or he'll be a different man altogether.' He gave her a mocking smile. 'But of course you wouldn't know that. I imagine you keep him quite happy, don't you?'

A wave of rage washed over her. 'I hate you!'

'Do you now?' He came a step closer, standing suddenly very close. 'Do you really?'

She turned away, her voice paralysed with fury. But he reached out to her, and turned her back to face him.

'I don't think you hate me,' he repeated, and his voice was quieter now. His hands were heavy on her shoulders and she could feel the warmth of his bare chest radiating on to her skin. Her heart was racing against her ribs with fear and anger.

'I hate what you say,' she said tightly. 'I hate what you do.'

There was a small pause. 'That's not the same thing, is it?'

She gave him a bitter smile. 'Close enough.' She held his gaze. 'At least we're even. You hate me, probably a lot more.'

'I don't hate you,' he said softly, too softly. 'I hate what you say. I hate what you do.'

She laughed, a cold, humourless laugh. 'You're blind and deaf.'

'Oh, no, I'm not.' He drew her closer, his mouth suddenly on hers. Their bodies pressed together and she had no fight in her. She didn't want to fight. He kissed every thought out of her head until she was nothing but a trembling bundle of nerves, her body out of control.

He withdrew quite abruptly, leaving her reeling. 'Funny, isn't it?' he said softly, but there was no mockery, no sarcasm in his voice.

There was no need to explain what was funny—she knew well enough. He turned his back on her to continue with his packing and she left the room, trembling, hating him.

Damn Marcus Penbrooke! Let him go to Africa! Let him stay there for the rest of his life and never come back!

She went into her room, threw herself on the bed and wept.

After he had left the days seemed to have lost definition. She felt like a zombie, moving through the days like an automaton. She didn't want to think; she didn't want to feel. She hated herself for being so depressed. Marc wasn't worth it. He was thousands of miles away and most likely she wouldn't see him again for years.

Then one day she was shocked out of her apathy by a phone call from the hospital.

Hayden had had a heart attack and was in the Cardiac Care Unit in a serious condition.

She hadn't thought things could get worse, but they had. For the second time in a month she was on her way to see someone in the hospital. The fear of losing Hayden tore her apart, twisting her stomach into a hard ball. In the past three years he had given her love and support, had been the father she'd never had. She wasn't ready to do without him. She drove to the hospital, trying desperately not to cry.

'Please, God, don't let him die,' she muttered, 'please, please...'

She was allowed to see Hayden for only a few minutes. She entered the room, her heart leaping into her throat as she saw him lying on the white bed attached to tubes and machines. An oxygen mask was strapped to his face, covering his mouth and nose. His eyes were closed and he looked grey and much too old.

Fear clutched at her heart, but she swallowed hard, forcing back the tears. The sight of this vital, energetic man reduced to inactivity and illness terrified her. She sat down next to him and took his hand. His eyes fluttered open.

'It's me, Daniella,' she said softly.

A smile crept around his pale lips. 'Damn nuisance, this, but I guess I can use the rest.' Under the mask, his voice sounded muffled.

She couldn't help but smile. 'I guess you're getting it whether you want it or not.'

'I can think of better things to do with my time than lie in bed.'

'I had a hunch you wouldn't be too happy here.'

'I'll be out of here in no time. Maybe you can bring me some work to pass the time; this is damned boring.'

She laughed, despite herself. 'You must be joking.'

He sighed and closed his eyes. 'All right, all right. I'll rest.'

She spent the rest of the afternoon trying to find a phone number for Marc in Ghana. Hayden's secretary at his office did not know how to reach him. She searched through desks and files to find information, to no avail. Hayden's lawyer's secretary was out for two days and could she call back later? She sat back, defeated. Think, she told herself. Think and be logical. What was the company name? Where in Ghana was it located? With whom had he been negotiating his contract in Washington?

Fifteen phone calls later she had a number. Daniella glanced at her watch—it was past midnight in Ghana. The number was probably an office number, not a private line, but she'd try it anyway. She dialled the operator, her hands suddenly shaking. Just thinking of hearing Marc's voice sent her heart racing.

Two hours later the operator gave up in frustration.

'I'm terribly sorry, but I can't get through,' she said. 'The operator on the other end says the phones are down in the town you're calling. Please try again tomorrow.'

After all the effort, she'd got nowhere. She gritted her teeth. Maybe a telegram would get through. Or did they travel over telephone wires? She couldn't remember. Well, it was worth a try, anyway.

Mrs Bell came in with a glass of iced tea. 'Any success?'

'No. The phones are down, or something. The operator can't get through. I'm sending a telegram; I've got to do something.' Her throat constricted. 'He looked so awful, Mrs Bell. What if——'

'He's not going to, don't even think it.'

'Marc should be here,' she said thickly.

Mrs Bell patted her shoulder. 'You're trying. It's all you can do, child.'

But was it? Three days later she still couldn't get through on the phone and the telegram had gone unanswered. Wasn't there anything she could do?

The good news was that Hayden was doing better. He was out of Intensive Care and in a regular room, reading the newspaper and teasing the nurses. The doctors were happy with his progress, but Daniella felt uneasy. Marc should know, she kept thinking over and over. Marc should be here. What if Hayden has another heart attack?

The fourth day she visited him, Hayden looked even better. 'Don't get any crazy ideas about letting Marc know I'm in the hospital,' Hayden warned her. 'Don't call him, he doesn't need to know.'

'Why not?'

'I'm perfectly fine, and I'll be home in a couple of days.'

'Well,' she said, 'I haven't called him.' Which was the truth. She had tried, but she hadn't succeeded. Yet she felt as if she'd lied to him.

He took her hand. 'You know, Daniella,' he said, and there was sad amusement in his voice, 'I'm a silly old man. I'm not very smart when it comes to things that really matter.'

'What do you mean?'

'I've made some decisions,' he said. 'I'm going to sell off parts of the business, consolidate the holdings and appoint someone to take over some of my responsibilities. I intend to start taking things a little easier. Do some travelling, maybe.'

Her throat went dry. He had made those decisions because Marc wasn't here to take over now that he had to slow down. Still, didn't Marc have the right to make his own decisions about the kind of life he wanted for himself? Yet Hayden's capitulation tore at her heart. Why couldn't those two talk this over between them? Why couldn't they respect each other, without the pain and anger that so clearly marked the tension between them?

'Are you sure that's what you want to do?' she asked, her eyes resting on his tired face.

'Yes,' he answered, his voice calm and determined. 'Very sure.' He smiled at her. 'Don't look so worried, sweetheart.'

Although Hayden's condition improved, her anger with Marc grew, aggravated by her frustration. She still couldn't get through on the phone and three telegrams had gone unanswered. Marc should be at home with his father, not in some Godforsaken part of the world where no one could reach him. Hayden was all right now, but what if he took a turn for the worse?

What if Hayden had died? They wouldn't have had the chance to make up. How would Marc ever be able to forgive himself? She looked down on Hayden's pale face. He needed his son now. No matter what had happened in the past, it was time they forgot and forgave.

There was only one thing to do.

She had to go to Africa and find Marc.

CHAPTER ELEVEN

TEMPORARY insanity.

It had to be. How else could she ever have ended up in this place? The heat, the smells, the flies. People shouting and laughing, all of them African. Men carrying baskets of squealing chickens, women balancing flat enamelled pans on their heads, carrying babies on their backs. Words and phrases of an unfamiliar language danced in the humid air. English was the official language of Ghana, so why didn't she hear it around her? The noise and general commotion overwhelmed her. Everything was strange and alien. Perspiration dripped down her back; her dress was soaked. She was losing her mind. She *had* lost her mind.

This was the bus depot, the taxi driver had assured her. Sure enough, there were buses, but Greyhounds, they were not. They were dusty and decrepit, but they moved, emitting noxious fumes. This is all I need, Daniella told herself, something that moves and gets me where I want to go.

She was tempted to crawl back into the taxi, go back to the hotel, back to the airport, back to Washington. But the taxi was gone. She took a deep breath. She could not go back; she had to find Marc first, for Hayden's sake. Damn Marc! Damn him for going back to Africa.

Damn herself for feeling what she did—this hopeless, mixed up mess of emotions that kept surfacing in her dreams.

Marc wouldn't be happy to see her, and her stomach

churned with anxiety at the thought of his cold grey eyes.
Why was she submitting herself to this? It was the cra-
ziest thing she had ever done.

'Madam, where you be going?' A young boy of about
twelve looked up at her with an expectant smile. He had
dark, intelligent eyes and smooth black skin. He wore
ragged shorts and a blue T-shirt that read 'Elvis Lives'.

'Kumasi,' she said, hoping she had pronounced it
right.

He nodded. 'OK, you come. I help you.' He picked
up her suitcase and began to weave through the crowd.
She followed him hastily. He stopped at one of the buses
and put her suitcase down.

'This one goes to Kumasi?' she asked, just to be sure.

'Oh, yes, madam, you no fear.'

That's easier said than done, my friend, she said
silently, groping around in her bag for some money.

Later, as she sat on the bus, careening along narrow
pot-holed roads full of treacherous traffic, she decided
that fatalism was the only philosophy that made sense
for the moment. There was no going back; she could
only hope and pray that she would arrive in one piece.
She could make herself sick with fear, or she could look
upon this as an adventure.

So, heck! She was having an adventure. At least until
she found Marc.

The small, dusty town north of Kumasi where the second
bus dropped her off lay baking in the afternoon heat.
After seven hours on two different buses, with no air-
conditioning and no suspension to speak of, Daniella
was ready for the adventure to be over. Physically she
felt more dead than alive, yet on another level the artist
in her was very much alive. All day she'd taken in the
colours and noise around her, feeling her creative juices

flowing. Watching the sights and the people, she'd felt her fingers itch as her imagination stirred up wonderful paintings glowing with life and colour.

The bus took off in a cloud of dust and she was left standing in another lorry park, this one much smaller than the others. A woman with a flat pan of mangoes on her head swayed past her. A little boy tried to sell her Chicklets chewing gum. Children stared at her and giggled.

She had no idea how to proceed. She looked again at the piece of paper with the address; at least she'd made it to the right town, alive and well. It was a miracle of sorts.

A dilapidated car stopped by the road. A young man waved at her. 'Madam! You need taxi?'

She scrutinised the rickety vehicle. It had nothing to indicate it was a taxi—no lettering, no numbers. Well, she could not afford to be picky. She moved up to the car.

'This is a taxi?'

The young man grinned. He had a great set of teeth and wore a clean blue shirt, open at the neck. 'For you, madam, it is a taxi.'

'That's what I thought,' she said drily.

'Where you be going, madam?'

She glanced down at the paper in her hand. 'Kaiser Engineering on Nkrumah Road,' She glanced up. 'Do you know where that is?'

He laughed. 'Everybody be knowing where that is, madam.' He leaped out of the car and took her suitcase. 'Please, you get in. I take you there.'

'Is it far?' The town did not appear to be a major metropolis. Across the street, two-storey buildings leaned wearily against each other. A goat wandered down the middle of the dusty road.

'Oh, no, madam, not far.'

She got into the back seat and watched out of the window as the man took off with dizzying speed. Once she'd had fantasies about living in Africa with Marc, painting wonderful, exotic pictures. She'd dreamed of going back to Washington a couple of times a year with a large collection of paintings. She'd take them to her agent, which was really a fantasy—back then she wouldn't have been able to get an agent. Now, after the success of the show, she would. Only now it was no longer relevant. She sighed. Long ago dreams, faded into nothingness.

The Kaiser Engineering compound lay on the out-skirts of the town. It took only a few minutes to get there and as they drove through the compound gates, she felt her heart thumping against her ribs.

The driver stopped in front of the main building. She paid him, climbed out and dragged the suitcase to the door, which stood wide open. She knocked and went through, entering a reception room. An African girl sat behind a cluttered desk, typing. She stopped and smiled at Daniella.

'Good afternoon, madam,' she said. 'May I help you?'

She had a pretty face, perfectly made up. Her hair was neatly parted and braided and she wore a crisp green and white striped shirt-dress. She looked clean and minty-fresh.

Daniella felt as if she'd been through the wars with her wrinkled dress, dirty and sweaty from the endless bus ride. Her hair hung in damp peaks around her face and she was sure her make up—or what was left of it— was smudged and smeared. Her skin felt sticky and was covered with a film of dust.

She ran her hand through her hair. 'I'm here to see Mr Penbrooke,' she said.

The dark eyes gleamed with curiosity. 'Mr Penbrooke has travelled, madam. I think he has not yet returned.'

Daniella's heart sank. 'When are you expecting him?'

'Yesterday, but he did not come. Perhaps today.' She reached for the telephone on her desk. 'I check for you.' She spoke into the telephone in a different language and laughed.

Great, Daniella thought. What am I going to do if he's not here? She thought of the poor, ramshackle town, wondering if it sported a hotel.

The secretary put the phone down. 'You are being lucky,' she said. 'Mr Penbrooke, he arrived one hour ago.'

Daniella expelled a sigh of relief. 'Where is he?'

'At his house.' She stood up, a little unsteady on her high-heeled green shoes. 'I shall find Joseph; he will take you to him.'

Joseph was a young man in tight jeans and a blue T-shirt. He took Daniella's suitcase and she followed him through the compound, passing some nondescript buildings of grey cinder block and several storage sheds with equipment, until they reached a group of bunga-lows lounging in the shade of tall coconut palms.

Joseph took her to the first one. A Land Rover covered in red dust stood in the driveway. 'This be Mr Penbrooke's house,' he said with a grin. 'He be happy to see you.'

You'd be surprised, she answered silently. She smiled and took the suitcase from him. 'Thank you.'

Joseph turned and strolled back down the dusty road.

Her heart in her mouth, Daniella knocked on the door. She heard slow footsteps inside the house, moving to-wards the door. It swung open and an African man with greying hair looked at her quizzically. He wore a white shirt and white shorts and was barefoot.

'I'm here to see Mr Penbrooke,' she said.

He eyed her curiously. 'Come in, please.' He stepped back to let her pass.

She entered a large, colourless living-room and before the man had a chance to offer her a seat, Marc strode through the door. Her heart leaped in her throat. It seemed impossible to breathe.

Marc stopped dead in his tracks. He stared at her, pale silver eyes intense, unreadable, his body taut. The very air in the room seemed to quiver with tension.

'What the hell are you doing here?' he said.

CHAPTER TWELVE

HE was even darker than she remembered, his eyes light and penetrating. His hair was too long, as it had been when he'd come home. He wore a long, loose shirt of some exotic African material and he looked strange, yet familiar.

'You do make me feel so welcome,' she said mildly. She wasn't surprised of course; she had expected him to be less than delighted with her arrival. Yet at the same time the old pain tore at her again. She took a deep breath. She was not going to indulge in sentimentality.

'What brings you here?' he asked coolly.

'You don't know?'

He lifted his hands as if in defence. 'I'm afraid not.'

Her stomach tightened. Her heart began to beat a little faster. He didn't know. 'I tried to call you on the telephone but the lines were down, or something. I sent you three telegrams.'

'Telegrams? Why? What the hell is going on?'

'You didn't get them then?'

'I just walked in the door, half an hour ago. I haven't seen my desk. I was on trek for over a week.'

Well, that explained everything.

'Talk!' he ordered.

The man who'd let her in earlier came into the room with two glasses of water. She took one eagerly and gulped half of it down. She was parched.

'Are you going to tell me, or not?' Marc demanded.

She took a deep breath. 'Your father had a heart attack. He's all right though.'

176

'A heart attack?' The colour drained from his face.

'He's all right,' she repeated.

He put his glass on the table and dropped himself into a chair, his eyes unfocused, his expression one of disbelief and confusion. 'When did this happen?'

She sat down across from him. 'A week ago Thursday. He was in Intensive Care for three days. I tried to call you for days, but I couldn't get through and then I sent the telegrams and I heard nothing; I didn't know what was going on.'

'I was gone. Even if I'd been here, you wouldn't have been able to get through to me. The phone lines were down for ten days, or so I was told. They were functioning again yesterday.'

'I thought you had to know,' she said dully. She felt suddenly very tired. She drank the last of the water. She saw the muscles move in his face, the clenched hands. Despite everything she felt sorry for him.

'How's the prognosis?' he asked.

'He'll have to take it easy from now on. His heart won't be able to take another one.'

He raked his hand through his hair. He looked exhausted. 'I can't think,' he said. 'I need a shower.' He closed his eyes briefly, then opened them again and focused on her face. 'You look as if you could use one, too. How did you get here?'

'By plane, bus and taxi.'

He gave a crooked smile. 'Very brave, I'm impressed.' It sounded as if he meant it.

'I'm tough,' she said evenly.

'Yes.' He gave a ghost of a smile. 'I know.' He came to his feet. 'Well, we'd better find you a place to stay. I've got an extra room here, but it's not the Hilton.'

'All I need is a bed.'

'You'll want an air-conditioner, believe me.'

'Well, yes, that would be nice.'

'Let's see if the thing works.' He marched out of the room and she followed him down a gloomy passage, into a spartan little room that held a narrow bed, a small wardrobe and a straight-backed wooden chair. An ancient air-conditioning unit was built into the window frame and when Marc switched it on it started up with a hoarse rumble, shuddered precariously, then went on. A blast of cold air came her direction and Daniella let out a sigh of relief.

'So far, so good,' Marc said. 'I'll get Moses to make up the bed.'

'Moses?'

His mouth quirked. 'Not the one who parted the waters of the Red Sea, I'm afraid. This one scrubs the bathroom and makes beds.'

Despite herself, she smiled. 'Phew, that's a relief.'

'The bathroom is the second door to the left. Ladies first.' He rubbed his chin wearily. 'I'll go to the office and check my desk.'

An hour later she was sitting across from him at the dinner table. Having visions of soup with fish heads floating in them, she was relieved to find plain boiled rice and something that looked like a beef and vegetable stew.

He gestured at the food. 'Not gourmet fare, but passable. It's just beef, nothing to worry about.'

'Good, I'm famished.'

'Didn't you have any lunch?'

'The bus made a couple of pit stops, but I wasn't sure what was safe to eat, so I had some peanuts and bananas and a lukewarm Coke. I drank it from the bottle.'

He nodded. 'Good thinking.'

They said little while they ate, and she was relieved. Not surprisingly, Marc seemed preoccupied with his own thoughts. The instant coffee that was served afterwards was abominable, but she was past caring. They sat in the sitting-room with an overhead fan stirring up the air at full speed, but the heat was still oppressive.

'Now tell me,' he said at last, 'why did you come all the way here to tell me about my father?'

'I didn't know what else to do. I kept calling and sending telegrams and I got nowhere.'

'What did my father say about you coming here?'

'He doesn't know. At least he didn't when I left. Mrs Bell will have told him by now.' She grimaced. 'It won't make him happy; he didn't even want me to call you.'

'Before I forget...' He came to his feet and disappeared into the passage, coming back a moment later with a piece of paper in his hands. 'I found the telegrams you sent me, and there was one for you, too.'

She frowned. 'A telegram for me?' She glanced down at the paper he handed her, then unfolded it to read the message. It was addressed to her care of Kaiser Engineering and was sent by Hayden. Her body tensed. 'HOLD YOUR HORSES STOP,' it read. 'I AM NOT OLD STOP I AM NOT DYING STOP NEXT TIME YOU WANT TO GO SEE MY SON I WILL COME WITH YOU STOP LOVE HAYDEN.'

She stared at the words, reading them again, not knowing what to think. 'It's from your father,' she said, folding it and putting it in her pocket.

'Is he angry you came here?'

'No.'

He took a drink from his coffee. 'Why didn't he want you to call me?'

She shrugged. 'I don't know all the reasons. But he's a proud man and he's never been sick for a day in his life and I think it embarrassed him.'

'Having a heart attack embarrassed him?'

She gave a half-smile. 'I do believe he considers it a character weakness to succumb to physical imperfections.'

He frowned, his eyes brooding. 'So why did you come all the way over here if he didn't want you to?'

'I was hoping you'd come home. I think in his heart of hearts he wants you to come.'

He gave her a long, probing look. 'And because you think *he* wants me to come home, *you* want me to come home? Is that right?'

'Yes.' She felt herself tense under his intense gaze. He was trying to figure her angle, what her true reason was for wanting him back home. He didn't trust her; he would never trust her. It didn't surprise her; still it filled her with resentment. She felt her defences rally.

'Consider it a good opportunity to get yourself back into his good graces again,' she said coolly, 'and possibly back into his will in the process. It might be worth your while.'

His eyes narrowed. 'What do you know about his will?'

She gritted her teeth. 'Not a thing. He has never discussed it with me. But since you were so concerned to get rid of me I assumed you were worried about me being in the will rather than you, the rightful heir.'

'I don't give a damn about being in his goddamned will!'

'You could have fooled me.' Oh, God, she thought, here we go again. Why did I have to start this?

He gave her a steely stare. 'Apparently you don't care about his will, either? Or at least that's what you want me to believe.'

Her heart sank; she didn't want to have the same pointless discussion again. 'If I cared, why would I be out here? I don't need his money. I don't care about his money and I never did.' Suddenly she began to tremble, feeling her composure slipping. She was so tired, and the heat enveloped her like wet flannel. Her head ached and her eyes burned. 'I just want...' Her voice broke and tears filled her eyes. 'I was scared; I was more scared than I've ever been in my life. I don't want him to die! If he dies...I'll have nobody.'

For a long moment there was silence while he kept watching her. She felt like screaming at him.

'So,' he said at last, 'you came to find me because you think that my father wants to see me?'

'That's what I've been telling you!' She wiped at her tears with the back of her hand. 'I don't want him to die! I don't want him him to die with his only child on the other side of the globe, hating him! He lost his daughter, he lost his wife. You're the only one he has.'

'He has you.' The words were spoken without inflection.

'You're his son! I don't want you to have to carry the guilt with you for the rest of your life that you didn't make up with your father in time. I never had a father, you know, or at least I didn't know I did until a couple of years ago, and all he left me of himself was his money. I never knew *him*. He was never a part of my life, and no amount of money can ever make up for that.'

He grew very still. Not a muscle moved.

She stood up, trembling, no longer able to go on, tears running down her cheeks. She wanted to get away and she walked to the door.

'Wait,' he said.

She stopped, her hand on the doorknob.

'Your father left you money?'

'Yes.' She should have felt triumphant, knowing that he would finally realise how wrong he had been, that she had never lived off his father, that her car, her clothes, everything had been paid for with her own father's money. She didn't feel triumphant. She felt tired and angry and sad all at the same time. 'I never took a cent from your father,' she said tiredly. 'He made me a loan in the beginning to help me start art school and to buy clothes so he could take me out. I paid it all back, every last cent.' She wiped a damp curl away from her eyes. 'What he offered me was a place to call home, and his support and his love. And I accepted that because... because we both needed each other.'

Every muscle in his body was taut, his eyes an impenetrable grey. 'Why didn't you tell me?'

She gave a bitter laugh. 'I didn't owe you any explanations, Marc, and besides, you didn't believe anything I said. Whenever I tried to tell you something, you didn't believe me. You're mind was made up, and your judgement set in concrete.' She opened the door and walked out; the air inside was suffocating her; she couldn't breathe and she had to get away.

Yet there was no relief from the oppressive heat out under the night sky, either. There was no breeze, nothing to stir the air. She walked down the street, passed the lighted windows of the other houses. There was the smell of cooking coming from one of the other houses, something roasting on an open fire or a barbecue. Voices, loud and joyous, laughing. Music, rhythmic and alien, came blasting from an open window.

Footsteps came behind her, then an arm around her, stopping her. 'Please, Daniella, come back inside. We need to talk.'

Saying nothing, she let Marc lead her back to the house; there was nothing else to do but go back.

'You want a drink?' he asked when they were back in the living-room. 'I've got beer and Scotch—that's it.'

'No,' she said tightly.

'Some water?'

'All right.'

He went to the kitchen to get the drinks. Coming back, he gave her the water and sat down in a chair across from her.

'I had a telegram from my father as well,' he said. 'Here, read it.' He fished the slip of paper from the breast pocket of his shirt and handed it to her. She straightened it on her knee, her gaze flying across the lines. 'DO YOU HAVE AN EXTRA BED STOP AS SOON AS I GET THE GREEN LIGHT I'LL COME OVER AND SEE WHAT YOU ARE UP TO STOP IS ABOUT TIME I FOUND OUT WHAT MY SON HAS MADE OF HIMSELF IN THIS WORLD STOP YOUR NEGLECTFUL FATHER.'

She swallowed hard at the lump in her throat. 'He's had a lot of time to think about things,' she said softly, feeling hope rising. 'He told me he's going to take it easier, sell off parts of the business, do some consolidating.' She hesitated. 'He said he had come to the conclusion he wasn't very smart when it came to the things that really matter.'

He was silent for moment, drinking his Scotch, eyes dark and brooding.

'Maybe,' she went on, 'he's realising that your relationship is more important than his business.'

He studied her face. 'What do you think about what he's doing?'

'I think he's right. Business, money—it's worthless without love. Maybe if you go home you could sort things out between you.'

'Maybe.' He raked a tired hand through his hair.

She sat silently in a chair watching him sip his Scotch, trying not to notice the lines of fatigue in his face, the tired look in his eyes. She couldn't think of anything else to say.

'You never had an affair with my father,' he said at last. It was a statement, not a question.

'I tried to tell you that.'

'You were to him the daughter he lost, and he was to you the father you never had.'

'Yes.'

He closed his eyes briefly. 'I wanted to believe that so badly, but I couldn't. Then on St Barlow...I almost convinced myself. You seemed...different.'

'I wasn't different! I've never been different. How could you possibly believe I was your father's mistress? How could you not *see*?'

'Because it was the only thing that seemed to make sense. And because I'd believed it for all the time I was here in Africa, after I got the first set of pictures.'

'And because of Clarissa,' she added.

His mouth twisted bitterly. 'Clarissa blinded me. And it frightened me. I was never going to be so blind again and not see the truth when it was right in front of my eyes. I was never going to be deluded again, never.' He rubbed his chin again, an oddly helpless gesture. 'It wasn't hard at all to believe you'd gone for my father after I'd left. After all, *I* was a lost cause sitting in darkest Africa, but my father was alive and well and very wealthy. All I could think of was Clarissa and how similar the two situations were.'

'Thanks a lot,' she said sourly. 'Being thought of as another Clarissa makes my day.'

'What do you know about her?'

She shrugged. 'Enough.'

'You didn't do much to dispel that image when I first came back this spring. You put up quite a performance.'

'I was furious. I was livid! Your mind was made up about me and there was nothing I could do about it, so I was going to give you your money's worth.'

'You did,' he said drily.

'I gave you exactly what you expected.'

'Maybe it was what I expected, but it was never what I wanted.'

She sighed and looked down on her hands in her lap. 'I couldn't believe you took me seriously. I couldn't believe you didn't see straight through my act.' She looked up and met his eyes. 'I wasn't trying to make you believe me, Marc. I was trying to make you see how ridiculous it was.'

'As you said, I was blind and deaf and stupid.'

Clarissa had done a real job on him; his experiences with her had coloured all his perceptions. 'You must have loved her very much,' she said.

He cocked an eyebrow in surprise. 'Who?'

'Clarissa.'

He groaned and closed his eyes briefly. 'Clarissa was one of the biggest mistakes of my life. I didn't love *her*— I loved some glorified image of her, some image that had absolutely nothing to do with reality.' He looked up. 'I seem to have this perverse capacity to create false images of people.' He hesitated, then came to his feet. 'Come with me, I want to show you something.'

He led her down the gloomy passage into another room, spartan and dark like her own, only with one bright spot of colour on the wall across from the bed. Her breath caught in her throat and her heart turned over.

The dandelion painting, spilling its cheerful sunshine into the drab room. *Love*, the caption read in neat lettering on the edge of the matting. Her painting. The painting she had given him over three years ago.

'When I wake up,' he said softly, 'it's the first thing I see.' He paused. 'When I came back here, three years ago, I was hopelessly, helplessly in love with you. I was also trying to be realistic and sensible. You were starting a new life; you were going to make a success of yourself as a painter. How could I ask you to give all that up and come with me here? So I tried not to make what happened between us something big and important. Yet every time I looked at the painting I knew I couldn't forget you.' He closed his eyes as if the memories were too painful. 'Then the pictures and the newspaper clippings began to come in.'

She clenched her hands, forcing down a wave of anger and disgust. 'Who sent them?'

He grimaced wryly. 'A well-meaning friend.'

'Some friend.'

He shook his head in denial. 'It was not done out of malice; it was meant truly to warn me.' He sighed again, as if it were costing him a lot of effort to get his story out. 'You must admit, Daniella, that, by all appearances, the situation looked a lot less innocent than it was. You were an unknown quantity in Washington circles, and all the pieces fit beautifully to make a very ugly picture.'

Daniella sat down on the edge of the bed. She felt weak with fatigue. 'And every morning you looked at my painting,' she said dully. 'What did you think, believing all those lies and innuendoes?'

'I convinced myself that, again, I had allowed myself to be taken in by an illusion. That those few weeks we had together had been a beautiful dream, and that I had been blind to your true nature, as I had been blind to Clarissa's. I convinced myself that you weren't the girl I thought you were—the smart, gutsy, idealistic girl who painted beautiful pictures.' He sat down next to her on the edge of the bed, his eyes on the dandelions. 'Every time I looked at your painting I felt miserable. I couldn't reconcile in my head the girl who had painted the picture with the heartless fortune hunter I believed you to be.

Part of me didn't want to believe the bad stories, yet another part believed you had to be a very crafty fraud to be able to paint something so beautiful.' He groaned. 'Oh, God, I thought I was going crazy.'

His paused for a moment and his face contorted in a mask of pain and regret. 'Daniella,' he went on, his voice low and tortured, 'I did a terrible thing to you and I don't know what to do about it. I can tell you I'm sorry, but it seems hopelessly inadequate.' Grey eyes met hers and she saw in them a vast, hopeless despair.

She felt a lump in her throat, an ache in her heart. She fought new tears, her throat aching with the effort not to cry. She didn't trust her voice. Biting her lower lip, she averted her eyes, seeing nothing but the shimmering yellows of the painting.

'Daniella, please say something.'

She shook her head numbly. Her voice wouldn't work. She lowered her gaze and felt tears dripping on her hands in her lap.

'Oh, God.' It was a strangled sound. Then his arms came around her, drawing her close against him. 'Don't cry,' he pleaded. 'Please don't cry.'

A sob broke loose, then another; her control was gone and a flood of tears followed.

He held her tightly, stroking her hair, murmuring things she couldn't understand. Her tears spent, she leaned against him, exhausted. She felt relieved and peaceful and shockingly weak. He handed her a handkerchief and she mopped up her face and blew her nose, feeling awkward.

It had been a long time since she'd cried with such total abandon. 'I'm sorry,' she said. 'I didn't mean to do that.' Her voice still sounded thick.

'Don't apologise.' His arm tightened around her again. 'Do you remember the time when you first showed me the painting?'

She nodded. 'You wondered why I had titled it *Love*. Dandelions are just weeds, you said.'

'And everybody is always out to destroy them.'

'Yes,' she whispered. 'But they always come back.'

He tucked a curl behind her ear. 'Look at me, Daniella.'

She bit her lip and met his eyes. There was hope there and for a moment time stood still.

'Do you remember what you said then?' he asked softly.

She nodded wordlessly; her tongue refused to move.

'You said, "You can't destroy true love, no matter what you do to it."'

'Yes.' It was nothing more than a whisper.

'Do you still believe that?' There was a plea in his voice and she felt the tension in his body.

She reached for his free hand and he grasped hers as if it were a lifeline. Her eyes filled with tears again. 'Yes.'

She heard his slow release of breath, then the silver shine was back in his eyes. 'We'll start over,' he said, 'and we'll do it right this time.' His mouth touched hers in a gentle, life-giving kiss. 'I love you, Daniella.'

Joy sang through her blood, warming her, making her heart spill over with happiness and hope. She pressed herself closer, feeling the safety of his arms around her, smelling the warm, familiar scent of him. It felt like coming home.

'I love you too,' she said. 'Oh, Marc, I love you too.'

Watch out for Eve's story next month in THE IMPERFECT BRIDE.

HISTORICAL

STORIES · 1991

Bring back heartwarming memories of Christmas past,
with Historical Christmas Stories 1991, a collection of
romantic stories by three popular authors:

Christmas Yet To Come
by Lynda Trent
A Season of Joy
by Caryn Cameron
Fortune's Gift
by DeLoras Scott
A perfect Christmas gift!